DEVIL'S DEN

On the run from the law, Whitman Morris stumbles across a secret place named Devil's Den. He believes he can hide there undetected, but then his horse is stolen and he is captured by another hunted man, Alex Hobart. Circumstances throw Whit and Alex together and they join forces along with Alex's son, Timmy, to run from Bullhead City's Constable Henry Drake. But soon they must defend themselves against rangemen who have turned to robbery . . .

Books by Concho Bradley
in the Linford Western Library:

THE FLATHEAD COUNTRY

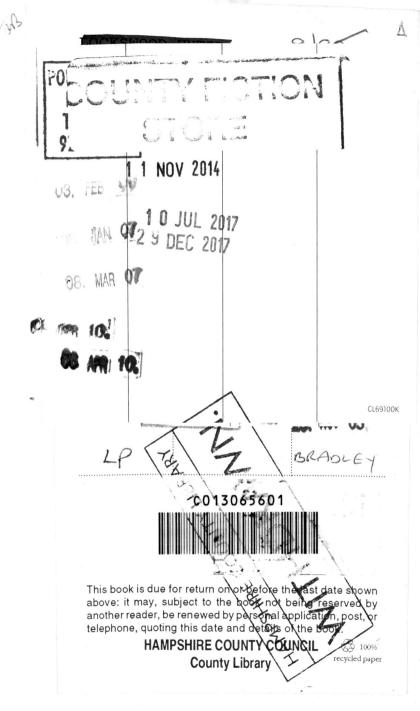

CONCHO BRADLEY

DEVIL'S DEN

Complete and Unabridged

LINFORD
Leicester

First published in Great Britain in 1997 by
Robert Hale Limited
London

First Linford Edition
published 1998
by arrangement with
Robert Hale Limited
London

British Library CIP Data

Bradley, Concho, *1916–*
 Devil's den.—Large print ed.—
 Linford western library
 1. Western stories
 2. Large type books
 I. Title
 813.5′4 [F]

ISBN 0–7089–5370–0

Published by
F. A. Thorpe (Publishing) Ltd.
Anstey, Leicestershire

Set by Words & Graphics Ltd.
Anstey, Leicestershire
Printed and bound in Great Britain by
T. J. International Ltd., Padstow, Cornwall

This book is printed on acid-free paper

1

A Secret Place

It was a wide, long mesa with a fringe of large old fir trees encircling it where the foothills gradually heightened to become mountains, high, rugged and massive.

The meadow itself was perhaps a hundred or so acres, flat, with stirrup-high grass, no brush, and a small cold-water creek meandering crookedly from east to west.

It was a paradise for high-country animals, deer, elk, an occasional moose, bear and ragged small bands of wild horses which had been driven to the high country with the advent of two-legged things and their cattle.

When Whitman Morris first saw it from an overlooking massif of close-spaced timber, rocks and shadows, he slowly dismounted and holding one rein, spent a quarter of an hour looking and wondering. If a man needed a secret place with natural blessings he couldn't have even imagined such a setting.

If other people had found it there was no trace. Homesteaders wouldn't stay, there wasn't enough farming ground, cattlemen wouldn't want a place where surrounding mountains had their share of varmints, bears, cougars, wolves and coyotes.

Morris hunkered beside his horse, whose concern was rest as it had been ridden hard for weeks. Morris rolled and lighted a smoke. If there was a disadvantage to this hidden place it had to be that searchers could approach unseen; the timber was old, massive and prevented penetration by sunlight.

The feed was rich, tall and a couple of months ahead of seeding out. Morris looked for trails; there were several places where trampled grass showed access from the sunless surround. They invariably led to water. There also were flattened places where animals had bedded down.

He led his animal out of the forest fringe to the meadow, hobbled it, left his riding gear in the grass, took his booted carbine and walked. The horse did not raise its head for a solid hour and then, with the sun on its back, stood hipshot dozing.

Morris had never been much of a walker so he rested often during an exploration which lasted until the sun was reddening in the west.

Southward, a goodly distance, he had made out two windmills and a collection of rooftops, otherwise his hike had revealed nothing threatening.

He returned to the meadow. His sound made the dozing, replete and comfortable horse open one eye briefly, then close it.

Morris savoured the sun's warmth while considering his animal. It was tucked-up-gaunt. They had been nine days floundering through mountains where feed was scarce. Before that they had covered considerable ground from before daybreak until after nightfall and while the mountains provided cover they also provided some of the ruggedest, untravelled country Morris had ever seen and he was not a mountain man; he had made his living since his teens in open grassland country. He was as good a stockman as they came. What made riding mountainous country difficult was his almost total lack of knowledge. Stockmen avoided dark uplands like the plague and even then they routinely lost cattle to predators.

As Morris sat in the grass he told the horse that the pair of them were about as out of their element as they could be. But, whatever this meadow was called — if it had a name — for the present it was a godsend.

They were both ridden-down and tucked up, the horse showed it more than Morris did. It was a largeboned bay animal with muscle and endurance to spare, otherwise they would never have got over and through the country behind them northerly.

He told the horse what they both needed was a month or two to recover and the horse hopped away to eat again. It was a pleasant sound, the horse tearing spring graze as sweet to it as roast meat was to its owner.

With the advent of dusk Morris made camp near the creek, propped his saddle gun against a stripling tree and luxuriated as naked as a jay bird in the creek, afterward sitting on a boulder to dry off.

In his saddle-bags he had salt, a tiny bag of flour that had baking soda mixed in it, a change of clothes and two cartons of bullets, one for the saddle gun the other for his hip-holstered six-gun.

He'd had two sacks of Bull Durham but had made his last smoke from scrapings. He had a razor with ivory handles and a whetstone, neither of which he had touched in days. His beard, like his hair, was bronze brown. He'd needed a shearing before he'd headed for high country. His beard was decently protective from sunlight but it itched, and once he'd found a large wood tick in it, after which he routinely examined it and although he would have liked to have shaved he had no inclination to do it where the only water was icy cold.

His camp was pleasant; at night the sound of soft running water put him to sleep before his conscience could get active.

His wariness diminished but not completely. Once, on his sixth day in the meadow, he hiked northward in the direction of a timbered ridge. It took the better part of the day to reach the topout. His legs and lungs were unaccustomed to on-the-ground activity.

From the rim he could see in all directions. To the east and west where high rims limited the view he saw nothing but more heavily timbered primitive country. Northward, the way he had come, there was a mild heat-haze but he knew most of the country and except for a stage-and-four bannering dust in its wake, he saw no movement.

South he could make out that pair of windmills and the scattering of rooftops. It was tantalizing; directly he would need supplies, but as he started back the way he had come he told himself all in good time.

He spent his thirty-seventh birthday cooking two mountain quail on an improvised spit above his rocked-around fire pit.

That evening, just ahead of dusk, he got his first scare. The horse, recovering fast, abruptly rattled its hobbles, stood stiffly erect, little ears pointing, and snorted.

Morris took the saddle gun, went into the northerly timber and stalked south as soundlessly as he could.

He saw the pair of cubs first. They were uninterested in the scent of the horse. They were rolling together in the dust of ancient fir needles, growling, spitting like cats and using their hind legs to kick with. If they scented the man or his horse they were too otherwise involved to heed them.

Morris used a mammoth old overripe fir tree for a shield as he stood, moving only his eyes for the mama bear and hoping for all he was worth he wasn't between her and her babies. There was no animal west of the Missouri River more dangerous than a sow bear with cubs.

When she came lumbering from the south-east Morris turned to stone, not only was she a good 7–800 pounds but she had torn ears and snout scars from many battles.

He briefly held his breath as the old girl paused to sniff before going to her babies and mauling them lightly to get their attention and, having gotten it, leading them deeper into the timber.

Morris would have shot her if he'd

had to but for two reasons he didn't want to. One reason was that she hadn't picked up his scent; the other reason was that the sound of a gunshot would carry even in heavily timbered country, and drawing attention to his presence was the last thing he wanted to do.

His only other visitors over the warm days were small varmints, some deer and an ugly bull moose, all in search of water.

The man-smell discouraged them: they could go up-country and water from the same creek.

He laughed at the horse. After the bear scare it would graze along and while chewing would peer in all directions. There were two highland predators horses instinctively knew were deadly, cougars and bears. The best horse on earth would have trouble eluding a cougar, but a horse didn't have to be inordinately fast to elude a bear.

Morris began to accumulate lard

under his hide and the horse began to slick up. Morris had no shoe pullers but if he'd had a pair pulling the horse's shoes would have helped only a little. Somewhere down the line he was going to have to get the horse fresh shod all around.

He'd been in the secret meadow almost two weeks when he saddled up and went meandering westerly and downhill a tad. He wanted to see without being seen. Unless watchers were out in the open country looking for movement they wouldn't have seen Morris and the horse. The sunless gloom would have seen to that.

He saw cattle from a considerable distance, and two horsemen, otherwise the farther he went the more timber made him sashay and eventually, with the sun dipping, he turned back.

As far as he could determine there was no one in his part of the territory, no homesteads, no ranch headquarters, no itinerant camp, only himself, the horse and a hundred invisible animals who watched him head out and head back.

One afternoon while emptying his saddle-bags he mildly wondered why there was no sign, not even of pot hunters. He was glad he'd seen no sign. But, in fact, along toward the end of the third week, he began to wonder why there were not even hunters. It was getting toward the time of year when townsmen as well as pot hunters began scouring out and around for winter meat.

He had a particular tree where he would sit and watch those distant cattle and that even more distant place with two windmills.

He wasn't getting restless, but he did need supplies. Living off game was fine, but it tasted better with salt.

By now he had a full russet beard. It was his most outstanding feature. Otherwise, his trousers, shirt, hat and boots were worn, faded and verged on disreputability. But that was not unusual among rangemen.

It was unusual among townsmen.

He finally rigged out, rode down a crooked game trail he had found, left the high country behind and rode about five or six miles toward those twin windmills. The closer he got the more of the village he could see.

A few hundred yards easterly there was the remains of a soldier fort; mostly the logs had been made off with, along with doors, windows, and whatever hardware folks could use.

The town had its share of log structures. Mostly, the logs were not old but now and then a leached-out log was visible, evidence of having been taken from the dilapidated old soldier fort.

There was a bullet-riddled wooden sign nailed to a cottonwood tree where a bridge crossed a piddling creek. The sign said, Bullhead City. Population Six Hundred.

As Whitman Morris approached the outskirts, past the bridge and sign, he wondered if that figure for the population didn't possibly include headstones in the cemetery off to the south-east, a fair distance from Bullhead City.

He didn't expect to find a smithy but there was one and judging by parked buggies and wagons it prospered. The blacksmith wore a riverman's collarless shirt was below average height and probably weighed close to 200 pounds. He didn't have much hair and when Morris hauled up out front the smith came out to consider the horse first then its rider as he said, 'Sure needs 'em all around, friend,' and shoved out a large, powerful hand. 'Elmer Barnhart.'

Morris shook the hand. 'Whitman Morris. You pretty busy?'

'Well, yes. How soon do you have to have him?'

'By evening?'

Elmer Barnhart nodded again, eyeing the horse. 'By closin' time, Mister Morris.'

Morris strolled northward, found the emporium and next to it the tonsorial parlour. He went there first.

The barber was a thin, tall, sour-looking individual. As Morris climbed into the chair something sticky touched his right hand. He looked at it as the barber swung his cloth. 'Dentist come through yestiddy,' he said, and offered no further explanation. 'You want the beard trimmed too?'

'Yes.'

'I got a bath-house out back.'

Morris said, 'Another time,' and watched people passing beyond the roadway window. Across the road was a tiny building with an oversized sign above the door: United States Post Office.

As the barber went to work he said, 'Damned sign's bigger'n the post office.'

Morris said nothing. Post offices had Wanted dodgers. Most government buildings had them.

The barber was so experienced at his trade he worked automatically, but unlike most barbers Morris had

14

encountered, this long drink of water said very little, right up until Morris put a two-bit coin in his hand while simultaneously scratching his neck. The barber said, 'They're lookin' for riders out at the Spencer place.'

Morris nodded about that and went out, turned south and passed the wide-flung door of the general store. It smelled good and aside from oiled floors and a noticeable dinginess, seemed to carry a more extensive inventory than Morris thought it would have for such a small community.

There was an overweight man near the back of the store who did not look up when Morris entered. He seemed to be working over papers and a ledger.

A woman appeared. She stood behind the counter without speaking or smiling. Her age was anyone's guess but she had silver pigeon wings of grey above her ears and her hair was pulled straight and was bunned in back.

Morris wrote on a scrap of paper what he needed and the woman went to various shelves to fill the order. When she had the supplies on the counter she said, 'Chewin', mister?'

Morris shook his head while making a slightly apologetic smile. 'No ma'am. Never could handle it.'

The woman threw a look in the direction of the hunched figure in the shadows and seemed to raise her voice a notch as she said, 'Filthy habit, chewing.'

Morris nodded. He wasn't sure she was right but it was nothing worth discussing. Over where the head and shoulders of the hunched man sat, he looked up, growled and went back to whatever he was doing.

Morris went to the café. It was a building with only a moth-eaten old Indian blanket dividing it from the next-door leather works. The proprietor was a young woman with skin the colour of pale silver. She had the blackest hair and eyes Morris had ever seen.

The special of the day was antelope

hash, fresh-baked bread and coffee.

Morris watched the woman walk back beyond her doorless cooking area. She was as attractive from the rear as from the front.

A pair of large gruff men entered, ignored Morris, went down the counter, sat and one bellowed in the direction of the doorless kitchen area. The woman called back and the same man who had bellowed spoke to his companion in a quieter voice.

'Dennis said it don't matter.'

His companion, with a battered constable's badge on his shirt, said nothing until their coffee arrived, then he stirred in sugar as he spoke.

'It'll matter if he shows up here.'

The gruff man passed that off too. 'Hell, Adam, he'd go westerly, maybe easterly.'

The woman brought their food and slid a third platter in front of Morris without raising her eyes to any of them.

Morris ate, sipped coffee and ignored

the pair of large men, even when the gruff man said, 'You figure out about Dennis's stole milk cow?'

The constable chewed and swallowed before answering. 'Not exactly but I will. No real cattle thief'd steal a milk cow?'

Morris paid up, smiled at the unsmiling woman and went outside. The sun was sinking but still high enough to show a huge world of flat to rolling grass country.

A stockman's paradise. He rolled and lighted a smoke, studied the town and went up to the pool room. He had better than an hour to kill before getting his horse.

2

A Missing Horse

When the horse was ready, Morris led it as far as the post office, looped the reins and stepped inside. The south wall was plastered with dodgers. He was looking at them when a small, fat, officious individual wearing a blue eyeshade called from behind his grille, 'They're all up there. Them as ain't I got in a box.'

Morris gave acknowledgement by nodding while he gazed at a particular Wanted poster. The face looking back was clean-shaven and hatless. His hair was black in the picture. It was actually bronze-brown.

He went back to his horse, made sure the supplies were evenly balanced, swung up and rode out of Bullhead City.

Several miles northward where he left the stage road, he encountered an old Mexican driving four milk goats with the aid of a dog and a tall stick. As they passed and nodded, the old man said, 'Don't go up there,' and wagged a finger. *'Fantasmas.'*

Morris drew rein. If there was one thing he knew about northern New Mexico it was that it was a place of endless myths and superstitions. He said, 'Where?'

The old man waved with his stick. 'The mountains. They are up there. *Mala hombres, fantasmas, espectros, aparecidos.'* The old man rubbed his chin, rolled his eyes and said, 'Espooks.'

Morris considered the goat man. He was not only old he was clearly a believer. Morris said, 'Why would they be up there, *señor*?'

'Because, *gringo,* no one goes up there. They know.'

'Know what?'

'That there are dead men. They walk at night.'

'What dead men?'

His goats were wandering and the fat old dog who should have been bunching them was lying at rest near the old man's feet. 'I have to go,' the old man said, gestured with his staff and went shuffling to catch up with his goats.

Morris watched his back-trail from within the first stand of big trees. There was no one in sight. He rode up the same game trail to reach his mesa as he had used going down. Dusk was close as he hobbled the horse and watched it hop where the grass was thick.

Because the distant high peaks cut off daylight quickly, Morris had to finish storing his supplies higher than varmints could reach with visibility decreasing.

He made a small dead-wood fire that burned fiercely without smoke, made supper, listened to the mournful cry of a night bird, let his fire die as he sat Indian fashion outside the fire ring of stones smoking and reviewing what he had heard and seen since leaving his secret mesa. Of the old goat man he paid least attention. He remembered the sullen woman at the café as well as the pair of large, well-fed individuals, particularly the loud domineering individual.

He smiled over the stolen milk cow. What the constable had said was correct: no cow thief worth his salt would steal a milk cow.

He bedded down listening to the soft music of the creek and awakened hours later to the same music. While making his dry-twig breakfast fire he glanced out where the horse would be grazing.

The horse was not out there. He stood up, searching in every direction. The horse was nowhere in sight. He left the fire to scout and what he found was the hobbles lying in the grass. They had been unbuckled, something a horse could not have done.

He returned to the fire, drank coffee, scuffed dirt to stifle the coals, took his saddle gun and returned to the place where the hobbles lay, and slowly picked up the trail, which was not difficult in tall grass. Several times he made out clear impressions of fresh shod-horse sign.

The tracks led arrow straight into the timber on a westerly course.

Tracking in territory where fir needles were thick enough to be spongy underfoot was a slow process. For short distances the sign was evident, then came times when it was not, but there were two certainties: one was that the tracks led unerringly westward; the other certainty was that the horse was not moving of its own volition.

He paused often, seeking footprints without any luck, which did not necessarily mean his horse was not being led, it could mean whoever was leading the animal made no impression.

There was a third possibility: this one Morris accepted as fact. Whoever had stolen his horse had ridden it bareback out of the meadow.

He could not recall indications during his round-about scouting hikes seeing anything that even suggested he was not alone in the highlands.

With the sun directly overhead he sat on a punky old deadfall, to the consternation of chipmunks who lived inside the log, and rested.

Without the horse he was afoot in a country that appeared to be endlessly primitive, uninhabited and gloomy and which also seemed to be uphill no matter which way a man walked, especially a man who by nature was not much of a walker.

When he resumed the tracking, he emerged from the dark shadow world of forest gloom and encountered a vast treeless strip of land with stunted stands of dead grass.

Glass rock. He'd encountered it before, and except for the thin skiff of soil atop what lay below, there were no tracks. He crossed through the dead grass following sign that led directly into the westerly timber where sunlight did not reach down through stiff, intermingled fire-needled branches a hundred feet and more above.

He lost the tracks where he fetched up on the east bank of a busy creek where his shadow scattered fingerling trout in all directions.

The horse thief knew his highlands. Also, he was savvy in ways to elude detection. He had led the horse into the water.

For Whitman Morris the question was simple: which way did he go, upstream or downstream?

A glance northward showed increasingly tilted rough country. Downstream was thickly forested but gently sloping country.

Indians might live northerly in secret places, but instinct or something anyway, set him hiking southward. Secretive and reclusive hold-outs would not go anywhere they could see domestic cattle and perhaps their herders, let alone see windmills and distant rooftops.

Whoever had stolen his horse would know the animal required feed. Somewhere downslope there had to be at least lightning-strike clearings or possibly even a mesa like Morris's secret place.

By mid-afternoon he was able to see distant brightness. The forest remained gloomy. Somewhere ahead where sunlight shone would be at the very least, edgings of grassland.

He was resting on a round rock when a covey of big birds came upcountry squawking as they passed overhead. When he resumed the trail he moved with caution. Unless he was mistaken, as the forest at ground level became brighter there might be an end to his search.

There was, but not as Morris expected. He was watching the ground for a hint of where his animal might have left the creek when a man directly in his path spoke without raising his voice.

Morris looked up. The stranger was

neither young nor old and wore black suspenders which stockmen never wore but which were common among home-steaders and settlers.

The man had an old hexagonal-barrelled Winchester in both hands and also wore a shell belt and a holstered Colt.

He said, 'I got to hand it to you, Cowboy. Put the guns on the ground.'

Because the craggy individual did not sound threatening Morris made no move to disarm himself as he said, 'It was a long hike, mister. Where I grew up they hang horsethieves.'

The unruffled stranger nodded. 'They still do in this country. You know any horsethieves, mister?'

'I don't know 'em but I'd sure like to.'

'Put the guns on the ground!'

This time Morris obeyed, not so much because of the stranger but as to the way he had given the order. As he straightened up he asked a question. 'Why my horse, mister?'

'You was camped in Devil's Den.'

Morris hung fire. 'If that's what it's called, that isn't much of a reason, mister.'

'It is to me,' the stranger replied, stood thoughtfully studying Morris for a moment before speaking again. 'I'm not real strong on shootin' people unless they got to be shot . . . If you just walk back the way you come . . . '

'I need that horse. These here highlands wasn't made for walkin' an' neither was I.'

This time the craggy stranger hung fire. Eventually he said, 'You went down to Bullhead yestiddy an' come back with supplies. I figure that means you're goin' to stay an' I don't allow that. Trouble is, Cowboy, even if I give you back the horse an' you went down to Bullhead, folks'd listen to you an' that's somethin' I can't allow neither. You got any suggestions, or do I kill you?'

Morris stepped past his guns and sat down on a punky log looking at

28

the pale-eyed, rawboned man with the squatter braces holding up his britches. He had been startled when he looked up from watching the ground but that had passed. He was trying to figure out the stranger. He hadn't once raised his voice nor had he once removed the bent finger inside the trigger guard of his gun. He was expressionless except for his obduracy.

Morris took a chance. 'I'll buy back the horse, mister.'

His captor sighed. 'That wouldn't work, would it? You'd ride down to Bullhead an' . . . '

'I'd ride easterly or westerly, nowhere near the town. Forty dollars for the horse and we never met.'

The craggy individual's eyes twinkled ironically. 'What's your name?'

'Whitman Morris. What's yours?'

The stranger ignored the question to ask one of his own. 'How'd you come to be on the mesa?'

'I stumbled on to it from the north.'

'You come across the mountains?'

'Yes.'

'Well, that's interesting. There's a stage road coupla miles east of Devil's Den. Did you know that?' When Morris didn't answer, his interlocutor continued to show that shrewd, ironic twinkle. 'That'd be one hell of a struggle, come over them mountains. A man'd have to have a real good reason for doin' that, wouldn't you say?'

Whitman Morris let go a noisy long sigh. 'Mister, I'm hungrier'n a bitch wolf. Forty dollars for the horse an' ten dollars for somethin' to eat.'

'You're awful free with your money, mister,' the other man said. 'That's fifty dollars. Gold or greenbacks?'

'Greenbacks,' Morris answered as he stood up off the log. Again the rawboned, craggy man spoke after a thoughtful long moment. 'Walk ahead of me, foller the creek. *Walk!*'

Morris walked. He knew the stranger was behind him but could not hear him for an excellent reason, he was wearing moccasins not boots.

It wasn't a long hike but to Morris, whose legs had been bothering him before he met the stranger, it seemed long.

The house was made of logs with a dirt roof from which sprouted grass. His horse was in a round pole corral eating and did not raise his head as the men passed. There was a brush pen about eight feet tall. Morris couldn't see them but he heard wild turkeys and piping mountain quail. An old dog was asleep on the porch protected from sunlight by an overhang. As they passed a soddy barn, a cow bawled and Morris's stride faltered. The man behind him said, 'Toward the barn, Cowboy.'

When they entered, an owl, larger than a chicken, dropped from the pole rafters and did not make a sound as it flew out the doorless front opening.

The rawboned man gestured with his rifle in the direction of a rough-hewn bench outside what Morris assumed was a harness room although excluding his horse he had seen no other horses.

As he sat down and looked up, the stranger leaned his rifle aside, wagged his head and removed a twist of tobacco from a pocket, whittled off a piece and considered Morris while putting up the clasp knife but still holding the twist of tobacco.

In anticipation Morris shook his head. 'Never was man enough,' he said.

The stranger tucked the cud into place without taking his eyes off Morris. He expectorated once before speaking in the same, unruffled tone of voice he'd used since they'd met. 'I'm goin' to make a guess, Mister Morris, an' you tell me whether I'm right or wrong. You was on the run when you come over the mountains.'

A large rooster, reddish brown, appeared in the doorway and considered the men from one eye without turning its head. It had spurs close to four inches in length.

The craggy man spoke again. 'At

least you didn't try lyin'. All right, show me that fifty dollars an' we'll go eat.'

Morris's problem was that the money was next to his hide under his shirt in a doeskin belt. He stood up. 'I got to pee.'

The craggy man nodded, 'Out behind the barn. Mister Morris, there's twenty-seven wolf traps hid under leaves plumb around the place. If you run an' get a broken foot or ankle I'd have to shoot you because there's no medicine man closer'n Bullhead City.'

Morris went out behind the barn, groped inside his shirt for one of the pockets, drew forth greenbacks, tucked his shirt back in and returned to count out fifty dollars and hand them to the craggy man, who watched fifty dollars being counted out and who spoke without raising his eyes. 'Have a good pee, did you?'

Before Morris could reply, someone spoke from out back where he leaned in the rear barn opening.

'Pa, he's got a money-belt under his shirt.'

Morris turned as the other man was folding the greenbacks and stuffing them into the pocket of his worn and stained trousers.

The person partly in shadows toward the rear of the barn was a lanky, rawboned, darkly tanned youth. Because Morris could not see him well he made a guess that the person in shadows was in his twenties. He was in his teens.

The soft spoken man said, 'Timmy, this here is Mister Morris. Mister Morris, that there's my son Timmy.'

Neither the lad nor Morris nodded although they looked at each other.

The pale-eyed man said, 'Let's go eat,' and as they were leaving the barn he also said, 'My name's Alex Hobart.'

Timmy entered the house last and went directly to the kitchen. His father jutted his jaw in the direction of a handmade chair and groped inside a handmade low cupboard, brought forth an earthen jug with a corn cob in its spout and said, 'It's not like the whiskey at the saloon down in Bullhead City, but it's passable. I make it out of corn.'

Morris took the jug and held it. He was not much of a drinker. On the other hand, under the circumstances, he slung the jug over his shoulder, removed the cob, turned his head and swallowed twice.

As he was handing back the jug his eyes spilled water, his throat closed and his stomach somersaulted. His host also took two swallows before putting the jug back where it had come from. He eyed Morris as the lad made noises in the kitchen. 'I told you it wasn't as good, Mister Morris, but we keep it in case of snake bites. Take off your hat an' get comfortable.'

Morris not only had fire behind his belt he also felt it in his toes and the ends of his fingers.

When the lad called them to eat Morris's first few steps yawed. His host appeared not to notice. As they sat where platters of food had been set, Alex Hobart said, 'I never could cook worth a damn, but Timmy's got a born talent an' for a fact he likes to cook.'

The lean, lanky lad smiled shyly at Morris as he took his place at the table. 'It'd be harder but for that stove pa bought from a mail-order house. It's castiron. We liked to killed ourselves gettin' it up here.'

Morris was sympathetic. 'I expect it was. Bullhead City's a good seven, eight miles.'

'We took delivery on it from Brandon, sixty miles north-west. We don't go near Bullhead City.'

Morris and Hobart exchanged a look. Morris had not only seen no harness horses but he'd seen no wagon. If they'd brought that iron stove sixty miles on their backs they must have taken weeks to get it here.

After eating, Hobart took Morris out under the overhang and said, 'I don't know what to do, Mister Morris, kill you or what. Care for a chew?'

'No thanks.'

'I don't care about the money in your belly-belt. We got almost no use for money. It's the other thing that troubles me.'

Morris gazed out where a high palisade of saplings surrounded a large garden plot and beyond the garden was a stretch of cleared land, five or six acres Morris thought.

Hobart spoke again. 'I got a notion that might work. Tell me what you think, but first off let's talk straight out. You got a price on your head?'

Hobart had said money was useless to him. Morris had to hope he was being truthful about that because there was in fact a $500 price on his head. He nodded without speaking and the pale-eyed craggy man spoke again.

'Devil's Den's a fair place to hide out but sooner or later there's men go up there. What I been ponderin' is if you moved in with Timmy'n me you'd be hid proper. Hasn't been no one come on to us in years until Timmy stole your horse to set you afoot so's you'd leave . . . care for another go at the jug?'

Morris could answer that question without any hesitation. 'No thanks. I was never much of a drinkin' man.'

Hobart got that faint ironic twinkle in his eyes when he said, 'I'd never have guessed that,' and they both smiled.

Timmy came out carrying an old lightweight, longbarrelled rifle. His father said, 'Be back before sunset, eh?'

The youth nodded, threw Morris a self-conscious smile and left the porch heading in the direction of the palisaded garden plot and the hay field beyond.

His father watched him out of sight and said, 'His ma died ten years an' seven months ago. I'm not much to read but I taught him. I'm better at sums. I taught him that too, but . . . '

Morris chose to change the subject,

personal revelations had always made him uncomfortable. 'You ever catch anythin' in them wolf traps?'

Hobart nodded. 'Now'n then. Gettin' back to the other thing . . . '

3

The Unexpected

It required a day for Morris to ride back to the secret mesa, get his gatherings and ride back. The sun was low when Alex Hobart and his boy watched Morris approach. As Morris looped reins down at the barn, the elder Hobart arose, winked at his son and said, 'That's two pelts you owe me.' Timmy had bet his father Morris would not return.

There was a small log storeroom which smelled strongly of hides that Alex Hobart guided Morris to and while standing in the doorway he said, 'You can air it out. Rats're a problem. Supper'll be ready directly.'

Morris stood with his back to the closed door. There was no window so he'd have to leave the door open.

40

While the smell was not particularly trouble-some to him, he would have preferred not to have it. Otherwise the small room was adequate to someone who'd been living out of saddle-bags.

He went to the house when Timmy whistled and although there was light it didn't come from the customary coal-oil lamps, it came from candles.

After supper, the three of them went out to sit beneath the overhang. Timmy mentioned a cub bear he'd seen yesterday afternoon and when Morris asked if the animal had been fat enough the boy answered slowly, 'He wasn't no threat to me. He sort of sat down an' just looked at me an' wrinkled his nose. Most likely he'd never seen a person before.' Timmy paused. 'He wasn't more'n maybe a year or two old. I told him to stay away from hereabouts an' tossed a rock. He run off.'

Alex Hobart offered an explanation for what was bothering Whitman Morris. 'We don't kill except to eat an' right now we got plenty.'

Timmy looked at his father. 'Tell him about the time we found that cougar in the trap.'

Hobart made a deprecating gesture. 'He don't want to hear about that,' and changed the subject. 'Mister Morris, you got someone lookin' for you?'

'I don't think so. Them mountains would turn back anyone in their right mind unless they had to cross 'em.' Morris rolled and lighted a cigarette and both Hobarts watched the trickling smoke. 'I went down to Bullhead City for supplies, Mister Hobart. There was my dodger on the post-office wall, except I had no beard an' my hair isn't black.'

'How much bounty?'

'Five hundred dollars.'

There was a long silence through which Morris knew exactly what they were wondering but wouldn't ask. He made it easy for them.

'I drove stage for a company up north for almost a year. I got to know exactly when a money pouch come from Denver to the bank down at Fort Collins. I made the haul six or eight times. Then I took out of the hitch the only combination horse, turned the others loose, told the two elderly folks who was passengers I was goin' back to Missouri, took the pouch an' left the coach in the middle of the road. I got no idea what happened to the rig, the horses or the old folks, but I guessed when the stage was hours overdue they'd send someone back to find out.'

Hobart said, 'Missouri?' and Morris smiled. 'Like I said, I'd been takin' the Denver pouches south for about a year. I had it pretty well worked out. Maybe they'd telegraph Missouri authorities an' most likely they'd track me. Not goin' east, goin' south toward Mexico.'

Hobart shifted in his chair, shoved out long legs and solemnly considered his clearing for a while before speaking. 'If they tracked you they'd come into the mountains.'

Morris nodded. 'If they did I figure they give up. If I'd been them I wouldn't have tackled them mountains.'

'But they'd figure you was goin' south.'

'All the time I spent in that hidden mesa, I never saw a soul.'

Hobart sent Timmy for the jug. In his absence, the craggy, pale-eyed man said, 'You figure they give up?'

'Well, maybe, but that dodger in the post office down yonder means they ain't forgot.' Morris blew out a ragged breath. 'I'm real obliged to you for your hospitality, but I'd best keep movin'.'

When Timmy returned, his father removed the cob, hoisted the jug, swallowed a couple of times and raised his eyebrows. Morris shook his head so Hobart put the cob back in and placed the jug beside his chair. As he was straightening up he said, 'The mountains is wide and deep, Mister Morris, but there ain't many clearings like Devil's Den. There's creeks everywhere; what there ain't much of is horse feed . . . You had a saddle, Mister Morris; that horse you taken off the coach was in harness.'

Morris nodded while gazing into the settling dusk. 'Stole it. Bridle, blanket with saddle-bags off'n a horse tied behind a saloon in a place I come on to. If it had a name I don't know what it was an' didn't spend time findin' out.'

Hobart cleared his throat. A cow bawled and he sent his son to milk it and Morris asked a question. 'When I was at the eatery in Bullhead City, a pair of fellers come in an' one said somethin' about a missing milk cow.'

Hobart cleared his throat again. 'When a man's got a son he don't want him to know his pa's a thief . . . I walked all night an' that danged cow didn't lead worth a damn.'

'Timmy saw it in the mornin'?'

Hobart said, 'I lied, Mister Morris. I told Timmy it maybe got lost somehow an' I found it wanderin' in the hills. You know how to churn, Mister Morris?'

'No sir; I never done it but I watched my mother do it years back.'

'While my wife was alive I helped her churn, make cheese'n butter an' feed the whey to piglets an' all. We needed a cow, Mister Morris.'

'That was a long walk.'

'All night an' then some, an' by the time I got her up here her neck was maybe stretched a mite but she now knows how to lead.'

'Is she branded?'

Hobart gave Morris a look. 'No. I didn't come down in the last rain, Mister Morris.'

Because Morris had put in a long day he was tired and dusk had turned into a moonless night. He arose and pushed out a hand. 'I been called Whit since I was a button, Mister Hobart.'

The pale-eyed man also arose. 'Same with me; it was Alex.'

Morris went down to the small log storeroom, flung out his blanket roll and this time put the canvas ground cloth over him instead of under him. The floor was dry *caliche* as hard as rock.

For the ensuing three days he helped in the vegetable garden. Four days after that he swathed hip-high wild timothy for hay. After the mow was full he went hunting with Timmy whose father remained behind for his own reasons.

Timmy was not a real hunter but he knew the country. Twice he allowed does with spotted fawns to flee out of range and once when a hen pheasant burst in wild, noisy flight practically underfoot, Timmy did not raise his rifle. When Morris looked at him Timmy pointed to the ground and the half-hidden nest with nine eggs in it.

With the sun beginning to slant away, they paused beside a piddling creek, sat in grass and shared a sausage as dark as original sin which was tough, flavoured heavily with garlic and required more chewing than eating. Timmy held it up. The sausage was not in a casing, it had some kind of mesh wrapping. 'Pa makes 'em,' the lad said. 'Good, ain't it?'

'Real good,' Morris agreed. He had a dozen questions but asked none of them.

They finished eating and dozed in tall grass under a westerly-moving sun. Out of the clear, Timmy asked a question.

'Is that what you got in that belly-band, the loot from the stage?'

Morris nodded as he dozed.

Timmy's next remark sounded almost defiant. 'Me'n Pa don't need money. Now we found that cow what with everythin' else we don't need nothin' . . . well almost nothin'. We can't grow ammunition for huntin', and salt. There's a lick some distance but we get more dirt from scratchin' than salt.'

Morris tipped down his hat. He was at peace. 'You got livin' by the tail on a downhill pull, Tim.'

A half-hour later as they were hunting again the youth said, 'I miss Ma.'

Morris said nothing.

'Pa's a crack shot. Me, I miss more'n I hit. Do you know how to put up meat, Mister Morris? We hoard glass jars by the dozen. Come autumn we put up for winter. Mostly we brought the jars with us. They was Ma's.'

A raccoon larger than a house cat was engrossed in digging. It neither saw nor heard the hunters but eventually it raised up wrinkling its nose. Timmy said, 'Got a den close by with shoats in it. See them nipples. She's makin' milk.'

Morris was learning. He said, 'Too fat anyway,' and led off past the raccoon.

It was about time to turn back when a turkey gobbled and froze them both in place. Morris looked intently along the ground and among the huge old trees until Timmy brushed his sleeve and jutted his jaw upwards.

The bird was large with a beard that hung down a good eight inches. It had seen them from its perch high among fir boughs. It shifted its feet but made no attempt to fly not even as Timmy raised his rifle. Morris was starting to raise his carbine when the boy fired and missed. The old Tom hoisted himself into the air in ungainly flight. Morris shot once, feathers flew and the turkey came down hard.

Timmy looked less chagrined than surprised. Morris had shot the bird in flight. As they went to retrieve their kill, the boy said, 'You're a good shot, Mister Morris,' and his companion replied dryly, 'Anythin' that big is hard to miss.'

Morris slung the bird over his shoulder as they started back. Timmy was quiet most of the way but when they had the clearing in sight he spoke ruefully. 'This danged old gun belonged to my grandpa. Pa said he could bark a squirrel with it at a hunnert yards . . . Someday I want to get a better gun, one that shoots bullets instead of lead balls.'

As they came closer, the boy spoke

again. 'I'll show you where the traps is hid. Right now we're between two of 'em.'

Morris looked hard and saw nothing. Timmy smiled. 'They're hid under leaves.'

Alex Hobart was waiting. When Morris dropped the turkey he said, 'Older'n I am. Look at them whiskers. But if it's cooked long enough . . . Timmy?'

The boy took the turkey in one hand, held his rifle in the other hand and went inside. He leaned the rifle aside, took the bird out back, sat on a stump and plucked it.

Around front on the porch, Hobart pointed to a chair and Morris gratefully sat down. He was averse to walking even for meat.

Hobart said something that made Morris's weariness vanish in an instant.

'There was riders over in Devil's Den. Three of them. One was an old Messican. They scouted up where you camped. They picked up your sign and come within a mile of here before turnin' back.'

After an interlude of silence, Morris said, 'Suppose they hadn't turned back . . . Alex, I'll ride out come daylight an' I'll lay tracks for 'em to follow away from here.'

Hobart had had all afternoon to think about this predicament, including something similar to what Morris had just said. His next remark both surprised Morris and gave him a hint about something that old goat herder had told him some time back.

Hobart said, 'The wolf traps'd keep anyone from sneakin' up on us, four-legged or two-legged.' He paused. 'Remember what that old man told you down yonder, about dead men walkin' at night?' Hobart again paused. 'It don't take much to scare Messicans an' if your goat man was the old Mex I saw this afternoon, he was likely crossin' himself every few yards. What me'n Timmy figured out to scare folks off, keep them to hell plumb out of our territory, is echoes. You know what echo boxes is? Mostly they're used to catch game. We hid some in trees an' some on the ground. Trespassers hear what they say being said back to 'em, like someone was mockin' 'em. Aren't no dead men walkin' around up here. Your old Mex — you know how they are, bring in ghosts an' whatnot until they got a full-fledged fable established. There's no one up here except for a scary-acting little band of hide-out In'ians about ten miles off. That's all.'

When Timmy finished plucking and gutting the turkey, he appeared from inside carrying a bucket. He and his father exchanged a nod. It was milking time. In fact it was past milking time.

As Alex Hobart watched his son hike in the direction of the barn he picked up the conversation where he'd left off.

'Two of them riders was strangers to me. Big, hefty fellers on big hefty horses. They had booted carbines but they sure-lord wasn't hunters.'

'What did they do when they saw where I'd camped?'

'Poked around, studied tracks, muttered a little. One of 'em said somethin' about nail heads in the dirt meant someone up here was ridin' a fresh-shod horse.'

A rooster crowed, some penned mountain quail made a piping answer and the old dog raised its head briefly then let it back down.

Hobart said, 'I didn't recognize 'em, but then most likely I wouldn't if they're from Bullhead City. I been stayin' clear of down there for ten years.'

Morris dryly said, 'Except for sneakin' down there in the night an' borrowin' someone's milk cow.'

Hobart made a lopsided grin. 'Yeah, except for that.'

Morris watched Timmy coming from the barn listing to one side under the weight of his bucket. 'I better go,' he quietly said, and this time Alex

Hobart did not argue. He arose to go inside and return with the jug which he offered. When Morris wagged his head Hobart sat down, pulled the cob, swallowed twice, replaced the cob and leaned to put the jug aside.

Morris said, 'In the mornin',' and again Hobart said nothing.

It was a sombre supper. Timmy told the older men he'd set the gobbler to roasting first thing in the morning so they could have it for supper. His father nodded without speaking.

Later on the porch, Hobart said, 'If you're good at fakin' sign maybe if they return they'll follow. If you're not, I'll be waitin' for 'em the same as I waited for you.'

Morris made a smoke and trickled a faint cloud. 'I'm real obliged to you, Alex.'

Hobart used Spanish when he replied. '*Por nada, amigo.* If you're ever back this way stop by.'

Morris went down to stand in night-gloom looking at his horse. It was no longer tucked up. He considered its new shoes. If the men from Devil's Den returned to Bullhead City and hunted up the blacksmith . . . well, hell, Morris would give them sign to follow.

He went to the log house, left the door open and bedded down. For some reason he felt less hunted than lonely. He remained awake for some time. Hobart had done right well. Whatever his reason was for being reclusive was his business. Morris only briefly dwelt on reasons. There would be a good one, unless Alex Hobart simply liked to live rough. Morris had known people who liked living like that. In fact, the longer he lay awake listening to small night sounds the more he thought he would like a set-up like Hobart had, and there was one reason why he would be better at it.

Timmy. Someday the boy would have to leave the highland. Morris wasn't sure Alex had done right by the boy. When Timmy met the other world he wouldn't be prepared for it. He'd make out, most likely. He was smart and adaptable otherwise he wouldn't have adapted as well as he obviously had. He might even be ingrained enough to continue living apart.

Morris closed his eyes. His last thoughts had to do with playing bird dog, which he would do. It was possible the men from down below would not return. He would have wagered money the old Mexican wouldn't.

He grinned in the darkness. He hadn't heard of echo boxes since he'd been a child. The idea, and it worked more often than not, was for wild turkeys, quail, ducks and geese to hear echoes of their own voices and go investigate. It was like shooting fish in a rain barrel.

4

Between a Rock and
a Hard Place

He awakened to an overcast sky which
was a surprise. The weather lately had
been warm and clear. The clouds had
sneaked in during the night.

There was no light at the cabin as
he rigged out, swung astride and rode
without looking back.

The overcast made track-hunting
more of a chore than it otherwise
would have been but he knew which
way he had hiked and found the tracks.
It was more difficult to find the new-
shoe tracks of his horse because Timmy
had ridden by a more direct route.

If there had been a sun it would
have helped but he sashayed north
and south until he found what he
was looking for, dismounted to scuff

loose earth, remount and take up the trail from there.

It wouldn't be a perfect ruse; trackers might search closer in which case they would find his tracks coming from the settler's place.

He had to chance it that once they found his new tracks they wouldn't scout for other sign.

He had no idea where he was going except that it was northward until he altered course some miles along and veered easterly.

Twice he left the horse below, climbed to high places and watched. If someone was tracking behind him they had to be invisible because he neither saw movement nor riders.

There was an excellent chance that the riders Hobart had seen in Devil's Den were hunters, prospectors or just plain travellers, although he doubted they would be travellers.

If they'd scouted up his camp on the mesa it still did not have to mean they were man-hunters.

But for someone in his situation there was every reason to lay a false trail and remain unseen. He was satisfied that somewhere people would want to locate and arrest him.

The further north he rode the more rugged and inhospitable the country was. If anyone had explored these mountains it must have been ages ago. Several times when he saw large animals they didn't immediately flee, they stood and stared. Game critters who saw humans fled at first sight.

Alex Hobart was right about the terrain; there were miles of enormous trees, fir and pine needles carpeted the understory inches deep. There was no undergrowth worth mentioning, resin from conifers soured the ground. He came upon a number of creeks and stopped often to drink and rest. In his favour it was not hot so the animal sweated only minimally, mostly from traversing landforms that appeared to be uphill no matter which direction it went.

He was watched; no one in primitive country wasn't watched from secret places on the ground and overhead. He was trespassing on some creature's territory every mile of the way.

The climbing lessened when he turned easterly and paralleled the distant rims and peaks.

Finally, late in the day, he rode into a tiny wildfire clearing, swung down, set the hobbles, removed the rigging and let the horse crop grass, which it did as though each mouthful was its last.

Morris scouted, found one of those cold-water creeks, dropped flat to drink and raised up listening. There were sounds, there always were in high country, birds made most of them but there were other sounds, none of which was threatening. Morris lay back near the creek and eventually moved. He had settled over an anthill.

The second time he sought a resting spot he searched carefully.

The overcast seemed to be thickening

and getting more darkly ominous. What it accomplished was to make telling time by the sun impossible. What it portended was a cloudburst.

When Morris continued riding he watched for places to use as protection when the storm unloaded. What he eventually found was a rock field of many acres with boulders of immense size. What he sought among this jumble of massive rocks was a place where the rocks might be piled atop one another, and what he found was even better, a cave whose entrance was large enough for a mounted man to enter, but he left the horse outside, took his saddle gun and went exploring.

He didn't worry about trackers. Unless they were close which he knew from watching his back-trail they were not, he no longer had to consider them a threat.

When the storm broke it would wash out all his tracks, even the sign back down by the Hobart place.

The cave had a musty, sour smell.

Animals had used it since time immemorial. There were bones ankle deep in places. There were also blackened places where fires had been built. The cave had one inhabitant, a rattlesnake in process of shedding its skin, during which time it was blind. It either heard or sensed his presence and went into a paroxysm of rattling.

Morris could not see it, the farther he went in the cave the more difficult it was to see adequately. Even if the sun had been shining, daylight would not have penetrated to the depths of the cave.

He picked up a bone and pitched it in the direction of the hissing. He must have missed widely because the rattling was not interrupted.

He found the rattler by tossing pebbles and bones until he struck it and the rattling was momentarily interrupted.

He moved carefully until the sound was close enough, then stopped, squatted and squinted hard. What he eventually caught sight of in the darkness was movement. The snake raised its head to do as rattlers do, gently moving its extended neck and head from side to side.

He shot it and the gunshot in that walled place sounded as though it had been made by a cannon. Morris could only hear the ringing in his head.

He returned to the mouth of the cave where his horse considered him from a dripping face. It was raining.

He brought the animal inside, off-saddled and hobbled it. They stood together watching the world turn from threat to downpour.

Morris made a smoke. His horse stood statue-like looking out. As far as the man was concerned the storm was a blessing. Every kind of track would be obliterated within hours. He had an unpleasant thought; if he'd been certain there would be a downpour he wouldn't have had to ride steadily for so long.

The horse swung its head. Morris

said, 'But we didn't know, did we?'

Morris had a scant supply of food, the horse had nothing and eventually in the night, it got restless. Horses minded rain less than did their owners.

Morris got little rest. If it had been daylight he might have helped the horse find grass and left it hobbled there. Nighttime was different, rain or snow or boiling hot weather, there were meat-eating carnivores of all sizes in the kind of country Morris was in.

By dawn, with the rain dwindling, Morris gave up and led the horse in search of food. The sun eventually arrived, the world steamed and the horse ignored everything in its hopping hunt for either graze or browse. If it hadn't been very hungry it wouldn't have attacked undergrowth. Horses were not, except out of necessity, browsing animals, they grazed.

By late afternoon the horse was satiated. He had no difficulty finding water, and by then his back was dry so

Morris brought him back to the cave and rigged him out.

They had been travelling easterly and because Morris had no destination he was perfectly agreeable to continuing in that direction.

They rode until forest gloom deepened then continued until they found a glade. The horse never once looked up. It only hobbled to fresh feed when one place was eaten plumb down.

This time Morris put the ground cloth between himself and soggy earth.

The following morning the sun was climbing, there wasn't a cloud in the sky and his horse was standing hipshot soaking up sunlight with both eyes closed.

Morris was in country as primitive as any he'd ever seen. Only once did he find something familiar, one of his earlier camps made during his initial flight southward. It told him nothing except that he had crossed his earlier trail.

Beyond a mile or so he saw a coach

road from a topout. It ran north and south.

He'd had enough of primitive country to last a lifetime. He followed game trails until he reached the road, rode southward and rode into a posse of heavily armed riders coming upcountry. One large glum-looking individual held up his hand and Morris drew rein. Morris recognized the unsmiling man; he'd been with another large individual at the café in Bullhead City. He'd seen the worn old badge then and he saw it now.

'What's your name?' the unsmiling man asked, and Whitman Morris lied with a clear conscience. 'Roger Dunham.'

'Where you from, Mister Dunham?'

'Montana, down through Wyoming, heading for country where it don't snow hip-pocket high to a tall In'ian.'

The unsmiling man faintly scowled. 'I've seen you before — somewhere.'

An impatient posseman said, 'We're wastin' time, Henry.'

A second posseman leaned on his saddlehorn eyeing Whitman Morris. He said, 'Henry, that's him. I shod his horse. I don't never forget a face.'

The unsmiling man gazed steadily at Morris. 'I'm Henry Drake, Town Constable of Bullhead City. Mister, where is Alex Hobart?'

Morris hung fire before answering. 'Who?'

'Alex . . . mister, his boy described you'n your horse an' he said your name was Morris . . . Shuck that pistol!'

Morris watched two posse riders draw their sidearms, and dropped his six-gun.

The town constable repeated himself. 'Where is Alex Hobart?'

Morris was between a rock and a hard place. He answered truthfully, 'I got no idea.'

A posseman who had parted from his companions rode westerly a short distance and was returning when he called ahead, 'He was ridin' alone, Henry.'

The lawman sat a moment in silence then roused himself. 'Let's go back. We'll take this one with us.'

The blacksmith and two other outspoken individuals protested. 'We come this far, for Chris'sake. He's got to be up ahead somewhere,' the blacksmith growled. Another rider, holding a fisted six-gun in his lap, said, 'He ain't Hobart. We can chain him to a tree and pick him up on the way back. Henry . . . '

'We are goin' back,' the constable said, and gestured for Morris to ride in front of him. The possemen moved to make room, then sullenly fell in behind the constable and his prisoner.

It was a long ride in the kind of country horsemen could not make good time. About sunset, the constable eased up to ride stirrup with Morris and said, 'Where have I seen you before, mister?'

Morris wagged his head. 'Montana, Wyoming maybe?'

Constable Drake put a scorning look

on Morris and did not speak again until darkness was settling, then he said, 'How well do you know Alex Hobart?'

'Hardly at all. I stumbled on to his place when my horse got loose an' stayed a day or two. My horse was wearin' down.'

Constable Drake looked unwaveringly at Morris when next he spoke. 'You didn't by any chance know him some years back when him an' some other vengeful Secesh tried to assassinate the president?'

Morris's look of surprise was genuine. 'Constable, I didn't know him at all. Like I said, I just stumbled on to his place lookin' for my horse.'

The glum-faced lawman spoke again in the same monotone. 'You interested in a bounty, Mister Dunham? There's a price on Alex Hobart — three thousand dollars. The biggest bounty I ever heard of. Even Jess an' his brother wasn't worth that much.'

Morris's answer was slowly given.

'It's somethin' to think about.'

'We'll get him,' the lawman said. 'He likely knows the mountains but he's on foot.'

Morris was curious. 'Are you sure you're after the right man?'

'We got his boy, Mister Dunham. He'd know his own pa. What bothers me is he didn't change his name.'

'What'd the boy have to say about that?'

'Nothin'. He was scairt pee-less when we run him down.'

'How did you find him?'

'Your tracks. Where they cut northward some of us kept goin' like you done, some of us scouted up the fresher tracks. When he saw us comin' he forted up.'

'With the boy?'

'No. The boy was milkin' a stolen cow in the barn and run like a rabbit.'

Morris watched the country open up and level out. So much for wolf traps.

It was late and cold by the time they reached Bullhead City. No more than a handful of lights shone. When they halted out front of a livery barn, a stooped old man with a big nose and small eyes came out, looked and said, 'Henry, that ain't him.'

The constable and his riders dismounted, they were tired and disgruntled. Only two of them were riding livery animals, the others walked away leading their horses.

The elfin liveryman kept shaking his head as he followed the constable and his horse inside. 'He's older'n and heavier,' he told the town constable. 'I've seen him three times an' this ain't him.'

As the lawman held out his reins he said, 'I know that. Take the reins.'

The Bullhead City jailhouse was made of logs. Northern New Mexico was as different from the southerly country as night was from day. Most of its buildings were log structures. Morris was herded toward the jailhouse which was in the centre of the settlement. Across from it and slightly southward was the café where the sulky-faced woman had fed him.

Only one posse rider followed Whitman Morris and the dour lawman inside, and it was the bull-built, expressionless posse rider.

He remained with his back to the door watching Whitman Morris. Constable Henry Drake shed his spurs, dumped his hat, sat behind a scarred old table with clasped hands looking steadily at his prisoner. He said, 'Let's clear up one thing, Hobart's boy said your name was Morris. You told me it was Dunham. Which one is it?'

'Morris. Whitman Morris.'

'Why'd you say it was Dunham?'

'That was my mother's maiden name. I've used it now an' again.'

Over at the door the posse rider snorted. Constable Drake ignored that. 'Set down, Mister Morris. There's a bench behind you. Did Hobart tell you he stole that milk cow?'

'Like I said, Constable, I wasn't there long enough to get to know

73

Hobart very well.'

'That bushy-headed feller holdin' his gun in his lap owned that cow. Stealin' livestock can get a man hanged but I expect you know that.' Henry Drake looked at the posse rider. 'You might see if them others got back yet.'

The burly man went out into the night and closed the door after himself. Constable Drake eased back in his chair. 'Mister Morris, where are you wanted?'

It was one of those abrupt questions that required a simple answer, and when Morris said, 'Nowhere, I was just headin' south,' Constable Drake slowly shook his head. He arose and jerked his head for Morris to do the same. At the cell-room door he asked if Morris had a hideout weapon and when Morris gave a negative head shake Constable Drake took him into an unlighted musty-smelling small room and locked him inside a strap-steel cage.

Drake marched back, closed and locked the door from the office side and a slightly breathless voice spoke to Morris from the darkness. 'Did they find my pa, Mister Morris?'

It was only barely possible to make Timmy out in the adjoining cage. Morris said, 'I don't think so. They caught me northward on the stage road, four of 'em. I think another posse went over my old sign. I got no idea how many.'

Timmy answered quickly. 'Three. Our dog warned us but Pa was over at the house an' I was at the barn. They come into the yard loaded for bear. I run for it. There wasn't no way I could get to the house.

'There was some shootin', not very much. I stopped runnin' to get my wind an' a feller on a big pudding-footed sorrel horse come straight at me. I give up. He'd've shot me if I hadn't. He owned that cow Pa brought from down yonder.'

'How'd your pa escape?' Morris asked, and got a reply that surprised him. 'I don't know unless he went into the cellar we made before we made the cabin. There wasn't no outside way to get down there. The wall in the kitchen closet was on hinges. That's how a man could get down there if he had to.'

'Timmy, don't say nothin' about this to the town constable. They think your pa escaped, run off into the forest. I expect they'll keep lookin'.'

Timmy moved like a ghost, sank down on the edge of a wall bunk and spoke again, this time in a small voice. 'You know what they want my pa for?'

Morris sidestepped a direct answer by asking a question of his own. 'Was your pa in the Confederate Army, Timmy?'

'The Ninth South Carolina Foot. He never talked much about the War. He said one time the South warn't beat, it was overrun. That's all he ever said an' I never asked questions.'

Morris sought and found his wall-bed and sat down. He was quiet for a long time and probably wouldn't have broken his silence if Timmy hadn't asked another question.

'What'll they do with us, Mister Morris? That feller Pa stole the cow from was madder 'n a wet hen. He told the constable me'n Pa had ought to be hung for rustlin'.'

Morris tried to sound reassuring when he said, 'First they got to find your pa an' my guess is that's not goin' to be easy.'

Timmy lay back on his bunk making a barely discernible shadowy outline.

Morris did the same after shedding his boots, hat and shellbelt with the empty holster.

Not until morning were they fed and then the constable scarcely looked at either of them. Morris could hear growly voices in the constable's office.

The food was better than Morris expected. He and Timmy ate well. Timmy didn't touch his cup of black coffee but as Morris downed his cupful the lad said his father drank coffee but he couldn't abide the taste.

Morris grinned and scratched his beard. There were folks who didn't approve of coffee but he'd practically been raised on it.

Constable Drake came to take Timmy to his office. He did not even glance at his other prisoner. Morris wanted to caution the boy about what he'd say and had to rely on their conversation last night to believe Timmy wouldn't say too much.

Morris could hear those growly, mean-sounding voices without being able to distinguish what was being said. What brought him to the front of his cage, gripping the steel straps, was the sound of a chair going over backwards and a high-pitched, partially smothered outcry.

When the dour constable returned the boy to his cage, he had blood on his shirt which came from his nose. Timmy ignored Morris, went to his bunk, threw himself face down and cried.

Morris hadn't heard a man, even a

half-grown one cry since childhood.

He sat on a three-legged milking stool, the only piece of furniture in his cage and waited. It was a long wait. In fact the sun was making steel-bar shadows on the floor of his cell before Timmy stirred, sat up, felt for the water pail and shakily washed his face. The bleeding had stopped and the swelling began taking its place. Whoever had struck the boy had done it more than once. His nose was badly swollen, one eye would open only halfway and he had a split lip and several loose teeth.

When he faced Morris he said, 'I told them. They was beatin' me. I told 'em about the cellar.'

Morris's reply was quietly offered. 'Your pa's long gone from there by now. Timmy, was it the constable beat you?'

'It was the feller the marshal called Dennis. He owned the cow.'

'Did the constable try to stop him?'

'No. The blacksmith caught Dennis

from behind and flung him against the wall.'

Morris continued to perch on the three-legged stool with hands clasped between his knees. He knew what a man-beating was like.

Later when the constable brought their supper Morris leaned on the front of his cell and said, 'What kind of a son of a bitch are you? He's just a kid.'

The constable shoved their trays under the door, did not look at Morris and left the cell room without a word.

5

Back to the Mountains

Morris wouldn't speak when Constable Drake took him to the office, he sat on a bench looking at a broken chair with blood on it.

Henry Drake said, 'You can't blame Dennis Grant. That cow give his family butter'n milk an' cheese.'

Morris put his gaze on the lawman without opening his mouth. Constable Drake leaned on his table with clasped hands. 'I been tryin' to remember where I saw you before.'

Morris was silent.

Drake wagged his head. 'It'll come to me. Meanwhile I'll tell you I don't believe that story about you usin' your mother's name. Men don't change names for the hell of it. You're wanted somewhere, ain't you?'

Morris arose, went as far as the cell-room door and finally spoke. 'Is there a doctor in Bullhead City?'

Drake remained at his desk as glum looking as ever. 'We got one — when he's sober. You mean for the lad?'

Morris nodded.

'Well,' stated Henry Drake, 'we can't do that. If it gets around town Dennis beat the boy folks wouldn't like that.'

'But you do, you son of a bitch!'

The lawman's clasped fists stiffened. 'You better watch your mouth, Morris, or whatever your name is.'

'Stand up you miserable bastard.'

Henry Drake arose slowly, flicked loose the tiedown thong over his holstered Colt and said, 'You won't be the first feller got killed attackin' a lawman trying to escape.'

Morris's reply was brusque. 'Come from behind that table an' I'll make you eat that gun!'

Constable Drake neither moved nor spoke. He'd been in the profession of law nine years. He'd seen that look on prisoners before. He gestured for Morris to open the door at his back and simultaneously drew and cocked his six-gun.

Morris entered the cell-room, went down to his cage, stepped inside and closed the door. Henry Drake came along, snapped closed the large brass padlock, holstered his weapon and without taking his smoky gaze off Whitman Morris said, 'I'm goin' to remember where I seen you, an' make up a good enough story to hang you . . . you son of a bitch!'

Morris kicked the stool around and sank down on it looking past the strap steel into the dingy corridor. In the next cage Timmy spoke. 'Did they make you talk?'

Morris turned to look at the swollen, bluish and disfigured face of the lad and shook his head as he said, 'We're goin' out of here.'

Timmy's swollen eyes brightened. 'How?'

'I got to figure, but, partner, we're

goin' out of here, I promise you that!'

Later, with another day dying, someone came down into the cell-room carrying two trays. It wasn't the lawman, it was the sullen, dark-eyed woman from the eatery across the road.

At sight of Timmy she stopped stone still. Morris growled at her, 'Slide the trays under the damned door.' He was hungry. As she was doing this she said, 'What happened to him?'

Morris answered in the same growly voice. 'He got beat up in the constable's office.'

The woman straightened, ignoring Morris, looking at Timmy. 'He needs doctoring.'

Morris nodded curtly. 'I told the constable that. He disagreed.'

'He's only a kid,' the woman said, finally looking at Morris. 'Kin to you, mister?'

'Not exactly and that don't make any difference does it?'

'Henry did that?'

84

'He said a feller named Dennis Grant did it, ma'am.'

The woman's expression settled into its habitual hard look. 'He's three times the boy's size and weight.' She paused before also saying, 'He's a drunk, beats his wife, bullies folks . . . Shouldn't I ask if he can be doctored?'

'The constable'll lock you up too. He told me there won't be no doctor.'

The woman returned her attention to Timmy. 'Can he feed himself? I could spoon feed him through the bars.'

Morris's internal rage was atrophying. 'I'll feed him, ma'am, an' you better skedaddle before the constable catches you talkin' to us.'

It was good advice and the woman took it, but later when the unmarried glum lawman appeared at the eatery for supper, the dark eyed woman couldn't stop herself from saying the boy across the road should be tended to. Constable Drake ordered supper as though he hadn't heard, ate in silence and when he arose to trickle coins beside his plate he said, 'Eleanor, your business is feedin' folks; my business is to keep the law.'

She let him get to the roadway door before saying, 'He can't be more'n sixteen, Constable.'

Drake hesitated briefly before passing beyond and closing the door after himself.

In the morning he had to go north where a tracker had located sign of a large man leaving the Hobart yard and going westerly. He was afoot. Henry and his companions would be a-horseback.

Timmy had difficulty breathing until Morris told him to breathe through his mouth. It heightened Morris's fury when, during his period of feeding the lad through the straps of steel, Timmy winced because chewing was painful. Having several loose teeth didn't help.

Morris required a long time to fall asleep. It was Timmy but it was also something else. He remembered a large, strong man beating a boy about

Timmy's age with a harness trace. When he finally slept he didn't sleep well and awakened before daybreak. Listening to the boy's wet gurgling sounds as he slept made Morris pace his cage. He was not by nature a violent man but like all men the potential was there; looking at the boy and listening to him made his leashed anger simmer.

When the breakfast trays arrived, a slightly stooped, grizzled old man brought them and as he slid them under the door he said, 'Constable's gone on a manhunt. I mind the place when he ain't around. It's a job that requires a feller to exert authority, like a few minutes back when Eleanor come with the trays I sent her packin'. Can't have folks goin' in an' out when a man's filling in for the constable.'

Morris waited until the old man was ready to depart then said, 'You got a name, mister?'

'Wiley Sanders.'

'Wiley, come back here for a minute.'

The old man dutifully returned and watched with an open mouth and wide-open eyes as Morris pulled the money-belt from under his shirt, opened one pocket, withdrew the currency and while looking steadily at the old man said, 'Wiley, you ever have five hunnert dollars in your life?'

The old man shook his head without speaking.

'It's yours, Wiley. All you got to do is fetch the key an' let us out.'

Wiley's tongue made a slow sweep of his lips. He looked up from the fistful of greenbacks, considered Morris for a long time then without a word went up to the office, returned with a large brass key and unlocked both cells.

Morris put the wad of money in the old man's claw-like hand and offered him some advice. 'If you're here when the constable gets back . . . '

'I know; he'll slit my pouch an' pull my leg through it. I'm goin' down to Texas where I got kin. Mister . . . ?'

Morris smiled. 'We're right obliged, Wiley.'

They left the jailhouse by the alley door. On the way, Morris retrieved his six-gun from the wall peg where Constable Drake had hung it. He also took his booted carbine which had been leaning against a wall.

Sunlight made Timmy's good eye water. Morris handed him his bandanna and led the way southward in the direction of the livery barn. The sun was climbing and it was going to be hot but the livery barn runway was shady and cool.

The stubby, elfin proprietor was skiving out the forefoot of a bay horse and heard nothing until Morris pushed a cold gun barrel into his neck from behind.

He straightened up very slowly and twisted around. His mouth fell open. He stared from Morris to Timmy, closed his mouth and said, 'Boy, what happened to you?'

Morris cocked the six-gun. 'Rig out

my horse an' the best one you got for the lad. *Now*!'

The liveryman may have been old and bothered by arthritis but he didn't move like it. As he was handing over the reins he addressed Morris. 'I told that pig-headed lawman you wasn't Hobart.'

Morris handed the elfin individual two $100 notes for Timmy's mount and while Morris and the lad left by the rear alley the liveryman said, 'Well, I'll be gawdamned. I only give twenty-five dollars for that horse,' and went gimping up in the direction of the constable's office.

Timmy followed. His good eye watered copiously and he could not see at all out of the other.

Morris led them due west and didn't stop until the moon was high. They watered the animals at a willowlined creek and slept in tall grass for several hours before continuing westerly.

Timmy's good eye still watered but less than it had formerly done. He asked where they were going and Morris gave a cryptic reply. 'As far as I figure we got to, then we'll go north and try to find your pa.'

The following day Timmy's good eye no longer watered and the swollen, closed eye tucked back a little so that he could see out of it.

The swelling was lessening and most of its bluish tint was gone. He seemed to have pretty well recovered from the shellacking his body had taken and while he said little he seemed pleased to be free in the company of a man he had liked from their first meeting.

On the fourth day, as they were riding northward, they encountered an ancient homestead with a dilapidated set of log structures. What encouraged them to stop there were several trees whose fruit was ripe, in some instances over-ripe. They fed apples to the horses, ate pears themselves and with enough inside their shirts to sustain them for awhile left the homestead in the direction of the mountains and a lowering sun.

Timmy was young, the young recover quickly from injuries and bruises and while he went willingly with his companion he was too preoccupied with unpleasant thoughts to talk much.

Morris understood something about that too; Timmy's world had disintegrated; everything he had come to rely upon since childhood was no longer there. Once he mentioned the old dog, worried that it would either starve to death or be killed by predators.

Morris eventually turned eastward and after half a day saw landmarks he remembered. They would be more than a mile above the Hobart place when they covered enough ground northerly. Eventually he found indistinct signs of his own trail eastward. The sign had been almost wiped out by rain but occasionally he saw sign and when he thought they were about where he wanted to be they rummaged for a glade and didn't make camp until they found one with feed for the horses.

The moon was rising when they stopped riding.

Timmy looked almost normal. He acted normal and even talked a little more. He knew in another day or so they would be down where his home was.

He had a dozen questions which Morris answered as well as he could by avoiding direct answers when he had to. Timmy wanted only to find his father.

Before they bedded down in a benign warm night he told the lad beginning with the next day their horsebacking would have to be as wary as Indians. He did not say it was possible possemen would be scouring the uplands, particularly after the jail break down in Bullhead City. He didn't have to mention those things; Timmy understood that they were in country where discovery could get them both shot.

He asked Morris why, since they were only acquaintances and since this was really not his fight, he was helping, and got a slow answer from the man lying nearby in the grass with his hat over his face.

'I got my reasons, boy, an' besides I got nothin' else to do.'

It was not a satisfactory answer but it had to do. Neither of them brought up the subject again.

Morris was beginning to feel at home in the primitive country. He had not entered it from choice but rather out of compelling necessity and until he had come across the secluded meadow called Devil's Den he had considered leaving it behind as quickly as he could.

They spent a full day from sunrise to sunset warily seeking places high enough to enable them to see the cabin and its surroundings. They found many horse tracks where searchers had scoured the area for Timmy's father. It occurred to Morris that the deluge he and his horse had taken refuge from in the cave was probably the best thing that could have happened to Alex Hobart. Before the downpour, trackers could pick up his trail, after the deluge they couldn't.

They separated and scouted on foot. Near the end of the day Morris was satisfied that whoever had been scouring the highlands a week or so earlier, was now gone.

They approached the cabin by moonlight and a dog barked. Timmy grinned until his face hurt. He had been a child when his father had bought the dog for him. They had a bond that surpassed many bonds the boy would make in later life.

With a starveling thin moon they moved as close as the tree fringe north-east of the grainfield clearing. Morris relaxed a little. It wasn't anything in particular that made him do that, it was something 'felt'. The area up ahead was deserted.

The dog barked again and Morris had to growl at Timmy.

The lad's retort was brusque. 'He's

old. He can't hunt; he's too old to catch somethin' to eat. I'm right surprised he's still alive.'

Morris's retort was also brusque. 'From the sound of that bark I'd say he don't know how pitiful he is.'

It was more a feeling than it was visual observation that made Morris sense the homestead was deserted. He saw the old dog on the porch peering in their direction and mildly wagging its tail. Timmy said, 'He . . . I don't know why he didn't foller Pa, he used to go everywhere Pa went.'

Morris had a hunch. He took Timmy with him and walked in plain sight away from the timber to the centre of the hayfield, stood there a long time and watched the old dog. Its eyesight might not have been good but there was nothing wrong with its sense of smell. It stopped barking, stood like a statue and increased the tail wagging. Timmy said, 'I'd like to go talk to him.'

Morris did not say a word, he took

the lad by the arm and led him back the way they had come. Behind them the old dog gradually lessened his tail wagging. It was as though he couldn't understand the boy leaving.

They hiked about a mile, maybe a tad more until Timmy turned easterly and with Morris following, came to a stumped-over clearing. Timmy said, 'Pa didn't want to cut trees for the house close by. This is where he done the cuttin' an' limbin'.'

Dusk came stealthily as it usually did where huge old trees interfered. Morris sent the lad for their horses. The feed was poor but it was better than a snow bank.

He went among the rotting old stumps. The trees had been felled years earlier, the stumps with the least resin were deteriorated and wormy.

When Timmy returned riding one animal and leading the second one, Morris had already selected the place for bedding down.

There was no water but they had

made dry camps before during their wanderings. The main thing was that the horses could crop grass and the two-legged creatures could eat remnants.

Timmy thought they should go hunting in the morning and although Morris agreed he did not do it with enthusiasm.

Timmy also thought he knew where his father might have hidden out and mentioned the cave Morris had holed-up in during the storm. Again Morris nodded in an abstract manner.

Timmy picked up this and looked puzzled when he said, 'You losin' interest, Mister Morris?'

The older man smiled. 'Nope. Why?'

'Well, you seem to be thinkin' like maybe you'd like to be somewhere else.'

Morris continued to smile as he replied, 'Bed down boy. We got work to do tomorrow.'

Timmy piled brush and small limbs of trees to make a bed and while he was doing this Morris asked a question.

'Timmy, do you know what skunk weed is?' When Timmy didn't answer Morris pointed. 'That brush you dragged for bedding, the stuff with big broad leaves, that's skunk weed. By mornin' when the stalks've had time to bleed you're goin' to smell bad.'

Timmy considered his carefully constructed bed, reluctantly pulled out the softest part and took it out aways and left it. When he returned, Morris had already made a bed of tufted grass and was lying with his hat over both eyes and both hands clasped over his chest.

Timmy rearranged his bed and lay down. He listened. When Morris didn't snore and his shirt rose and fell irregularly Timmy spoke. 'It's a long ride to the cave. We'd best get an early start, don't you think?'

Morris answered from beneath his hat in three words. 'Go to sleep.'

Timmy slept, the night was warm and while a bed up off the ground and something to cover up with would have been preferable, it was not an option.

It was after midnight when one of the horses nickered and Morris sat up, dropped the hat atop his head and waited.

It wasn't a long wait, the man in moccasins didn't make a sound but his silhouette was moving, the only movement.

Morris quietly said, 'Come on in, Alex. Hope you brought some sausage with you.'

Hobart didn't smile as he came past his sleeping son and squatted with Morris. 'You done right well for a flatlander, Mister Morris.'

Morris smiled. 'A man looks after his critters, especially his dog. They didn't find your cellar, eh?'

'Oh yes, they found it. I was on a knob past the hayfield an' heard 'em callin' back an' forth when they found it. I didn't go back for two days. Like you said, a man looks after his critters.'

Morris gestured. 'Reach yonder an' wake Timmy.'

6

A Big Circle

Until dawn arrived Alex Hobart couldn't get a good look at his son. When he saw the fading signs of a beating he softly said, 'Who did it, boy?'

Morris answered. 'A posseman name Dennis Grant. It was his cow you stole.'

Hobart was gazing at his son when he said, 'It's my fault. I done somethin' foolish when you was a baby. I should've left you with kin when I had to run for it. But I couldn't sleep nights. Your mother had died on me. You was all that was left.'

Morris interrupted. 'The boy'll be all right. I'll take care of Mister Grant.'

Hobart shook his head. 'I got no use for anyone named Grant, Mister Morris, I'll see to it.'

Morris considered the craggy man nearby and said, 'I guess it don't really matter as long as someone yanks the slack out of him. By the way, Alex, I told you — my name's Whit.' He smiled. 'Now we got to find somethin' to eat.'

That proved less of a problem than Morris expected. Hobart led off on foot. He was accustomed to travelling that way and the following riders didn't have to slacken gait.

They stopped in a measly little clearing about half surrounded by enormous boulders and as Morris swung off he wasn't surprised: squirrels, chipmunks, even wolves and coyotes cached food.

As he led the way among the horse-high rocks Hobart explained. 'When a man's exploring over considerable distances he just naturally hides caches.'

The cache was in a rocked-over place where someone had chinked access with rocks and done such a good job of it that when they finally broke through, the food had not even any chipmunk tracks.

It did not surprise Morris either that the mainstay of the cache was homemade sausage encased in some kind of webbed cloth.

While they were eating Hobart said he hated the idea of having to abandon the homestead where he had raised his boy and where he had worked hard.

Morris sat in boulder-shade, chewing. When he could, he dryly said, 'There'll be other places, Alex. Even if you could stay there you'd have visitors. By now you're well known down in Bullhead City.'

Hobart again studied Timmy's face. He said nothing but he clearly thought a lot. When Morris spoke after an interval of quiet, he said, 'Another week or such, the lad'll be good as new . . . Alex, we got to figure where we go from here. I doubt that unhappyactin' town constable'll still be scourin' around. As time goes by somethin' else'll come along to fire up folks. They won't forget but my guess is that they'll lose interest. You ever been south to Messico?'

Hobart was wiping his lower face with a blue bandanna when he answered. 'Years back. It's a poor country with a lot of beat-down people in it.' He tucked the bandanna away before continuing, 'The life of a *norteamericano* isn't worth two bits. They'll kill a man for his boots, his guns, even his hat. Is that where you was headin'?'

'Yes, but now I guess not.'

'How about up north, Colorado, Wyoming? I been told it's good country.'

'It is, if you like snow inside your boots an' months of cold bad enough to freeze the . . . toes off a brass monkey. I can't go back up there.'

Hobart belched behind an upraised hand. 'That leaves east or west. You know the westerly country?'

'I sure don't an' what I like best I don't think it knows me.'

'We need another horse, Whit.'

Morris smiled. 'Moccasins 'd wear out before we got halfway.' He arose and dusted off. 'Let's go get us another horse.'

Timmy brought up the rear as his father led off southward. It helped that the landform tended downhill. When they could see beyond the trees a hot sun backgrounded miles of grassland with an occasional bosque of trees.

Cattle grazed, small in the distance. Hobart beckoned for Morris to dismount. When they were together the tough, craggy man raised a rigid arm. 'Barely in sight; you see that clump of trees? See rooftops down there?'

Morris nodded. 'Cow outfit?'

'Yes. Big one. They'd have horses.'

Morris nodded again. 'An' riders who'd shoot or hang a horsethief on sight.'

Hobart said nothing as he peered far ahead. Timmy came up leading his horse. 'Pa . . . ?'

'Yes, boy.'

'If we rode into town after dark maybe we could buy a horse.'

Both older men looked steadily at the youth until he reddened, mumbled something and went to stand on the off-side of his horse.

Hobart asked Morris if he'd ever stolen a horse and got an oblique reply. 'I borrowed the one I'm riding but that's about all. You . . . ?'

'It's been a long time. Back durin' the War; but that wasn't exactly stealin', it was a game we played with the Yankees. We'd steal, they'd steal back.' Hobart continued to squint southward. 'I'd say that outfit's a good two, three miles.'

Morris agreed, but to himself. 'Wait for dark an' leave Timmy waitin' until we get back.'

Hobart looked past Morris, understood the expression on his son's face and slowly, adamantly wagged his head.

They led the animals westerly until they found a creek, hobbled them, dumped riding equipment in the grass bordering the creek and made themselves comfortable. Timmy was hungry but said nothing. His father and Whitman Morris napped. Timmy didn't, he worried and fretted. He really wasn't cut out for the life of an outlaw or a fugitive, and he worried about his old dog. The idea of abandoning him stuck in his throat. He knew better than to mention it; the grown men would say it was part of the sacrifice that had to be made.

Whitman Morris surprised Timmy; he sat up without a sound, reached for his hat, ran both hands over his face and got to his feet, turned and nudged Timmy's father with the toe of a boot.

Alex Hobart washed in the creek, sent Timmy to fetch the horses and, during his absence, the craggy man said, 'It's botherin' the boy leavin' home.'

Morris nodded. 'When he's older he'll understand.'

'Whit, it bothers me too. I raised Timmy in this country. It's been good to us for a long . . . '

'All right, Alex, we'll stay. But we still need another horse.'

Hobart nodded, picked up his hat, hitched his shellbelt and holstered sidearm into place and when his son returned with the horses Hobart told his son he and Morris had decided not to flee, they'd stay in country the father knew better than the back of his hand.

Timmy was relieved but simply said, 'Someday we can go home; you reckon?'

Hobart didn't trust himself to answer so he simply nodded.

When his father and Morris rode away through the forest and the night, Timmy followed until he lost sight of them, then went back to wait.

It would be a long wait.

There was only a hint of a moon, which was favourable. The night warm. They eventually started up cattle from their beds and once heard the thunder of fleeing horses without catching sight of them. Since neither man carried a lass rope it wouldn't have made any difference if they got close.

An owl sprang from the grass with a mouse in its talons. Morris's horse bunched to shy. Morris rattled reins and spoke. The horse freed up and continued southward.

When they were near enough to see lights, there were none. Closer still they could make out the buildings, the corrals and a number of half-grown trees in the yard. Hobart said, 'There'll be dogs,' and Morris nodded, but they came around to the west where using horses heard or scented them in a pole-breaking corral, built round so there'd be no corners and with a wide pole gate. For whatever reason the dogs did not erupt; it might have had something to do with the fact that the log barn was between them and the yard.

Hobart leaned to dismount and Morris put a hand on his arm, shook his head, swung down and softly said, 'Keep watch.'

Morris entered the big old barn seeking a length of lead-rope, found several hanging from a nail and returned to the corral.

Hobart saw the shank and nodded approval. If his companion had never been a horsethief he certainly understood how it was done.

The gate was one of those large handmade ones with a long pole from ground level to the top of the hinged side. They were built that way to minimize sagging. It only worked while they were new.

Morris lifted the gate after tossing the harness-snapped chain aside. The corralled using horses eased away and bunched up. Morris chummed his way toward the closest animal, considered it briefly and moved toward another animal, a close-coupled buckskin which, like most of its kind, had a short back and an unforgiving spine. It was like riding a jackhammer but successful horsetheft had to be accomplished swiftly, especially in the yard of a large cow outfit that had a bunkhouse full of seasonally hired riders.

The buckskin led well. Morris came out of the gate with him, handed Hobart the shank, swung up and turned back the way they had come.

They had cleared the yard, were something like a hundred yards on their way when all hell broke loose back in the yard. It wasn't just fiercely barking dogs but the corralled animals came out the gate Morris had left open sounding like a stampede.

They were well on their way when Hobart looked back and saw lights in the main house as well as the bunkhouse. He sat forward and told Morris they had better rawhide it. Morris was willing and boosted his mount over into a lope. Hobart cursed and took dallies. He had encountered something buckskins were noted for: balking.

Morris swung back, got behind the balking buckskin, swung his reins high and brought them down. The buckskin

111

sprang ahead. Each time he hung back Morris hit him. They made fair time but not as good as men leading a stolen horse wanted to make.

The buckskin was stubborn. He only reacted favourably when Morris hit him. Hobart swore and held his dallies. They had covered about a third of the distance toward the distant uplands when the sound of running horses became audible. Morris hit the recalcitrant buckskin and Hobart heeled his mount. With no choice the balky buckskin broke over into a lope.

The horses they heard in their rear were gaining. Morris was ready to yell for Hobart to cast loose the tie rope when three horses ran past several yards to their left. It was the animals from the corral; they were running free.

Hobart yielded a little slack, the buckskin, knowing what would happen if he hung back, loped easily beside Hobart's horse.

By the time they reached the timber where Timmy had heard them coming, both men were sweating although it was late enough in the night for it to be cool, bordering on being cold.

Morris made a squaw bridle of the lead shank, helped Timmy astride and led off westward. He wanted to cover enough ground so that the trackers would be unable to get them in sight.

The buckskin was well broke. His only vice was that balkiness when being led by someone a-horseback.

When dawn came they were in country which had been stumped over. Clearings were broad. Southward, the mountains pulled back and open country crept northward.

They stopped briefly to rest the animals and Alex Hobart walked southward toward a low land-rib. When he returned he said, 'Four of 'em with an In'ian tracker.'

'How far?' Morris asked.

Hobart was snugging up his cinch when he answered. 'They're still south of the uplands. I'd guess maybe three, four miles.'

As they resumed their way Morris asked if Hobart knew the country they were passing through and got a cryptic reply.

'Not real well. I hunted and scouted this far some years back but can't say I know it.'

Timmy was getting chafed. Riding horseback did that to a person if the animal they were straddling sweated, and the buckskin, obviously not accustomed to the kind of sidehill riding he'd been doing, was sweating hard.

The next time they halted was after working clear of the stump country northward into heavily timbered and boulder-strewn uplands. From there they had several opportunities to watch the backtrail. The four riders were still coming, more slowly because the tomahawk tracker was unable to make good time until he reached the stump country, then he moved faster.

Hobart said, 'They're gainin',' and led off eastward.

By the time the sun was climbing

they were back in country Hobart was familiar with.

Morris left them to work his way westerly seeking high ground for a sighting.

What he saw stopped him dead in his tracks. Their pursuers were hightailing it back the way they had come and six or seven bow-carrying Indians were watching them flee.

He went back and told the Hobarts what he had seen and Alex shook his head. 'I knew they were back in there; I saw their sign a few times, but I never figured they'd come this far south.' He was briefly thoughtful before offering a possible explanation. 'Game must be scarce up near the rims. I'd guess they'll get back to their hide-out country fast as rabbits.'

Morris was standing beside his mount when he dryly said, 'They was on foot. They won't get back up yonder as fast as them rangemen'll get out of the mountains.'

They led the horses for an hour or

more, until Hobart took them to one of those lightning-strike clearings where they freed-up the horses, went to a creek and both drank and washed.

Morris was drying off when he said, 'That's the first time I ever saw In'ians off a reservation,' and Hobart commented, 'Like I said, I've come on to their sign a few times, miles deep from here. I never saw one. Far as I'm concerned if it's a secret that's fine with me. If they don't bother us we won't bother them.'

They rested until sundown. Timmy asked if his father had another of those caches and the older man shook his head, smiled at his son and said, 'Can you find your way home from here, Timmy?'

The boy smiled. 'Blindfolded, Pa.'

'Then let's go down where we can make a decent supper.'

Timmy looked steadily at his father, the smile gone. 'They might be watchin' the place,' he said.

Morris arose from the grass, dusted

off and addressed the boy. 'I'm getting real tired of this runnin' all the time.'

They picked their way to the northerly highlands from where they could see the homestead. Timmy spoke anxiously, 'I don't see Shep.'

His father led off, Timmy followed and Morris remained in the rear and slightly off to one side. He did not believe they were actually running much of a risk. The log house, the barn, the cleared places were without any kind of movement. But it was a risk, and in fact the biggest one they had taken except for stealing the buckskin horse. When they broke clear of the timber Hobart didn't hesitate.

He rode directly toward his yard. As he was close enough to be heard the old dog came from beneath the porch, did not make a sound but wagged his tail.

Timmy left the buckskin at the tie rack out front of the barn. Dog and boy met midway The old dog licked and wiggled and licked some more. As

Timmy's father passed, Timmy asked if he could take his dog inside the house for something to eat. Hobart nodded.

Morris was at the tie rack when Hobart entered the house and swore loudly.

Morris crossed hurriedly, walked past the open door and stopped dead still. There were three wolf traps, the nearest one was no more than six or eight inches from the door. Hobart had come within inches of springing it.

Timmy appeared at the door with his dog. Morris turned. 'Don't come in. Don't let the dog pass you.'

They used sticks to spring the traps, tossed them out on to the porch and while Timmy's father searched the cabin Timmy went briskly to work in the kitchen, the old dog never more than a few feet away. He fed the dog before firing up the cook stove.

When Hobart had finished exploring, he got the jug, which was much lighter than it had been, and handed it to Morris. They both drank.

Morris wasn't as uneasy as he was cautious. He took his saddle gun and prowled outside, around the house, through the barn, threw grain to the quail and chickens, and found a cow halter on the floor of the barn. Dennis Grant had his cow back.

7

Visitors

The temptation was strong but they didn't linger. Before following Morris and his father, Timmy piled scraps from supper and other things on the porch. Rode away looking back. His old dog didn't raise its head; it was scarfing up food.

They were heading for a creek Hobart knew about a couple of miles from the cabin when a flight of startled birds sprang to life up ahead and flew past moving fast.

Hobart held up a hand, slipped to the ground and with the saddle gun in hand went scouting. Timber was not only thick but the tree trunks were large around.

Morris and Timmy dismounted and waited. It was a fairly long wait and when Hobart returned he wasn't alone; a large coarse-featured man was walking in front. He had an empty holster.

Alex told his prisoner to sit on the ground and to shove his hands down inside his britches as far as he could, which the coarse-faced man did as he stared steadily at Morris and Timmy Hobart.

Alex made a careless gesture. 'He was back yonder. His horse is tied to a tree. It has two big gunny sacks tied behind the cantle.'

Morris thought he had seen their prisoner before but made no effort to remember. He said, 'Two gunny sacks? Empty, Alex?'

'They're empty.'

Morris returned his attention to the large man. 'Lookin' for mushrooms, was you?'

The man hunched over because of his encased hands, nodded vigorously.

Morris went over and hunkered. When their eyes met, Morris was sure they had met before. He said, 'What's your name?'

The coarse-featured man offered a belated reply. 'Al Hitchcock.'

Timmy exploded. 'His name's Dennis Grant!'

Alex Hobart crossed to stand in front of the captive. 'Take your hands out'n your britches and stand up.'

Their captive didn't get completely erect before Hobart hit him, kept hitting him until the captive gave ground and held both arms high to protect himself.

Hobart stopped with both arms at his side. 'You know that boy yonder?'

The captive darted one look in Timmy's direction and shook his head. 'Never seen him before.'

This time when Hobart swung the captive had no time to raise his arms. The blow caught him along the point of the jaw and the captive went down like a pole-axed steer.

They sent Timmy to fetch the horse and, as it came into sight, Morris said, 'Mushrooms my butt. If I was to guess

I'd say he brought along them gunny sacks to carry off whatever he could steal from your cabin, Alex.'

Hobart was looking down when he said, 'I'll stomp the waddin' out of him, the no-good son of a bitch.'

Morris caused a diversion when he said, 'He likely didn't come alone.'

They left the captive where he was lying, got astride and picked their way soundlessly and carefully, each rider about five yards from the other. If their captive came around he couldn't go very far, Alex was riding his horse and leading the buckskin.

They made a wide sashay, found no one and no recent sign and headed back.

The captive was sitting up gingerly exploring his jaw. When he heard them coming he stood up.

He said, 'You'll never get clear. There's possemen combin' the mountains from the south an' Big Bow rangemen comin' in from south-east.'

Morris alighted as he said, 'You

know the feller who just shellacked you? He's the boy's pa.'

The captive considered Hobart from small, malevolent eyes. 'Cow-thief Hobart.' This time when Alex moved ahead the large man sidestepped. He was watching Hobart when he addressed Morris. 'Stay out of it. It'll be a fair fight.'

It might have been a fair fight if Timmy hadn't yanked the carbine from the boot on Morris's saddle and cocked it.

His father missed a step and his adversary twisted to look. He looked at Morris who was not holding a Winchester, flicked his gaze to Timmy and Alex Hobart waited, arms at his sides. Timmy said, 'I'd as leave shoot you as look at you.'

His father didn't raise his voice. 'Leave it be, Timmy. Ease off the hammer.'

The next moment he rushed the coarse-faced man and caught him too high, on the shoulder. Force half spun the captive, he continued to turn and made Alex miss his second blow, then the captive swung around and struck Hobart as momentum carried him past.

The captive was no novice. Morris thought now what the café-woman had said. Dennis Grant was a bully, a spoiler and worse words to that effect. She might also have said but hadn't was that Dennis Grant was a seasoned brawler.

While Hobart was off balance Grant went after him and positions were reversed, it was now Alex Hobart trying to protect himself and his opponent boring in like a cougar.

When Morris thought it had gone on long enough he caught the captive from behind with the barrel of his six-gun. Dennis Grant went down in a heap and Alex glared but said nothing. He had a flung-back streak of blood on one cheek and both hands were bruised.

Hobart said, 'I'll kill him, the . . . '

'Help me get him on his horse, Alex. I think he was blowin' smoke about riders comin' but if he wasn't we don't want to be where they could find us. Give me a hand, he's heavier'n a boar pig.'

Timmy helped. For a fact Dennis Grant weighed close to 200 pounds. Fortunately his horse didn't sidestep.

They were leaning on the horse sucking air when Morris said, 'If there is someone comin' from the south we dassen't ride down hill.'

Timmy piped up. 'If they're comin' from the south-west it'll be them rangemen the In'ians scairt off yesterday.'

Alex Hobart leaned off the horse to massage his hands when he said, 'Back to the cabin, then. We can fort up. If they want a scrap . . . I got plenty of bullets an' a pouch full of lead balls for Timmy's rifle.'

Morris wasted a long moment in thought before shrugging and mounting his horse. He held out his hands for the reins to Grant's animal and started riding.

Father and son rode on each side

of Dennis Grant to prevent him from falling. Morris had hit him a pretty fair lick. He didn't begin to recover until they were working their way through big trees and had the cabin in sight. He groaned and raised an exploring hand to his head. There was a smidgin of blood and a growing bump. He would have a headache he'd remember a long time.

Timmy had the captive's six-gun shoved in the front of his britches and when Grant turned slightly to eye it, Timmy's father spoke to him. 'I'd like for you to try it.'

Grant looked ahead.

Morris was not convinced they were doing the best thing. With hundreds of miles of primitive mountainous country behind them it would be better to have manoeuvring room. As they entered the yard Timmy's old dog was on the porch wagging its tail. Of the mound of food Timmy had left there was now only a greasy spot on the weathered floorboards.

When they swung off in front of the barn, Timmy took the reins to his father's and Morris's animals. As he was leading them into the barn he said, 'I'll get the other one directly then start dinner.'

Alex and Whit un-horsed their captive, took him deep into the barn and, using harness chain, made him fast to an upright. They then went out to the yard in the direction of the house without a word.

Inside, everything was as it had been. Hobart went after the jug. This time Morris shook his head. His stomach was like a sack with a hole in the bottom and that corn whiskey was powerful.

Timmy arrived breathlessly. When he entered the house he was clearly glad to be home. He smiled at the older men and went to the kitchen. His father sank down in an old chair, motioned Morris to another chair, shoved out his legs and said, 'I expect Grant was lyin'. There's no sign in the yard nor in the house that they come back after the last time.'

Morris had an instinctive feeling of being caged, otherwise he might not have said, 'Maybe he was lyin' about possemen comin' from Bullhead City but not about the rangemen.'

Hobart echoed Morris's earlier remark. 'Whit, I'm' tired of runnin'. If they come maybe they'll get supper but by Gawd we'll get breakfast. I built this house when there was still tomahawks skulkin' around. If we don't want 'em in here, short of a cannon they aren't comin' in.'

Morris responded to Timmy's call to eat like a striking rattler. Alex Hobart was close behind and whatever was on their platters was attacked without conversation. Timmy too ate like food was going out of style. He ate for two, himself and the patient old dog beside his chair.

Afterward while the boy was cleaning up in the kitchen, the men went outside, Morris to build and light a smoke, his companion to sprawl comfortably and skive off a cud of molasses cured which he tucked into one cheek. As he was pocketing the twist he said, 'I been thinkin', Whit. We been goin' in double harness for a spell. You told me what you done so I'll tell you what I done.'

Morris killed his smoke, settled to listen and although he already knew the substance of it, he let Hobart fill in the details.

'Years back when I was about Timmy's age I joined the Ninth South Carolina Foot under a crabby old goat named General Amos Strickland.

'We fought in Tennessee to southward and westerly.' Hobart paused to expectorate over the porch railing. As he settled back he did not speak for a long moment. 'I was about the youngest except for another lad named Robert Southal. He got hit by a Yankee sniper at a wide place in the road called Freeport, near a river.'

Hobart paused again. This time he

neither expectorated nor moved. 'I come late to the War. I wanted to go earlier but they told me they didn't take thirteen year olds . . . My pa an' uncle was killed along with my cousin, Reg. He was sixteen. That time when I volunteered they took me. Whit, we marched barefoot with a pocket of cracked corn an' a canteen. When it ended I had never seen so many Yankee blue bellies. It looked to me like there was millions of 'em. Well fed, plenty of wheel guns, supply wagons . . . I didn't surrender I snuck away. When that Yankee general named Grant become president . . . I was . . . I had some scores to settle, so I went to Washington to kill that whiskey-swillin' son of a bitch. I hung out around the White House an' didn't see him but twice; once he was goin' inside, the other time him an' some other men come out front to get into some buggies. It was too long a distance but I got off three shots. You never seen pompous bastards run like they did. All hell busted loose. A woman standin' nearby also watchin' looked at me an' fainted dead away . . . I run an' been runnin' ever since. Care for a turn at the jug?'

Morris shook his head, leaned back and shoved out his legs. A long silence settled between them. Eventually Alex spoke again. 'That was a long time ago, President Grant died in 1888 as two years later Timmy's mother died. After that I come West, went for a homestead patent on this ground an' you can guess the rest.' This time when Hobart leaned to expectorate he didn't lean back. 'An' now I got a Grant in my barn chained to a pole.'

Morris had watched their captive being chained. Hobart had left little room for Dennis Grant to move. He was as tired as a man got when sitting relaxed after an arduous day and no sleep the night before.

He arose. 'That sour-faced town marshal told me why there was a bounty on you. What bothered me at the time was why, if he knew, didn't he come after you long ago.'

Hobart arose to stroll toward the small, smelly storeroom with Morris. 'I didn't know he knew.'

'Only reason I can think of,' Morris said, 'is that maybe he only just found out. It was a long time ago, like you said, if there was dodgers out after all them years they'd likely been replaced by other dodgers, like the one on me with black hair an' no beard.'

They had almost reached the storeroom when Timmy called from the porch. They turned. The lad was pointing northward. It was three riders coming at a walk. Hobart shook his head. 'No one I ever saw before.'

Morris made a good guess. 'Lookin' for the buckskin horse.'

Both men walked toward the barn where Morris untied Grant's animal, led it inside to be off-saddled and turned it into a stall where there was a full manger. The horse had been a long time with nothing to eat. It buried its face in the timothy hay unmindful of the arrival of other horses or anything else.

Morris and Hobart leaned on the tie pole as the horsemen came up. One of them was a bull-necked man with swarthy skin. He nodded from the saddle. 'Name's Beckwourth. We lost a buckskin horse. There was tracks. By any chance you gents seen it?'

Hobart was about to reply when a horse fight erupted behind the barn in the corral. After the racket subsided, Whit Morris addressed the bull-necked individual. 'Good animal was it, Mister Beckwourth?'

'We got better ones, friend,' the swarthy man replied.

'What would you say the buckskin was worth?' Beckwourth's forehead got a slight crease. 'It ain't mine; it belongs to the outfit we ride for.'

'Would you reckon they'd sell it?' Morris asked.

Beckwourth's frown deepened. 'They likely would. Why?'

'If I offered you a hunnert dollars for it . . . ?'

Beckwourth stared and a thin rider behind him said, 'That halter-pullin', iron-backed son of a bitch . . . take the money, Beck, the old man wouldn't care if we told him we couldn't find it.'

Beckwourth continued to regard Morris, wearing a slight frown. 'Do you have the horse, gents?'

Hobart lied without taking his eyes off the mounted man. 'It drifted in. We found it upcountry a'ways in a clearin'.'

Beckwourth's scowl deepened. 'Did you for a fact. Gents, two fellers stole that horse out of a corral at the ranch we ride for. We tracked it here.'

Hobart nodded. 'My boy found it an' rode it home.'

'Where is it?'

'In the corral out back. You heard 'em squealin'.'

The bull-necked man leaned to dismount and Whit Morris said, 'Stay

135

up there. Like your friend said you didn't find the horse. Didn't even see it. Take the money an' go back the way you come.'

Beckwourth's companions stared at his back. The thin one repeated himself. 'Beck, take the damned money.'

Another rangeman spoke. 'Beck, the season's about over. We'll be let go within the next week or two. As far as I'm concerned I'd use that buckskin for wolf bait. Take the money.'

Beckwourth looked steadily at Whit Morris. 'You got a hunnert dollars, mister?'

Morris fished forth a crumpled wad of greenbacks and began counting. When he was finished he said, 'That leaves me thirty dollars.' As he went close to hand the swarthy man the hundred dollars, the thin rangeman said, 'You must want that worthless damned horse real bad, mister.'

Alex Hobart replied. 'My boy's taken a shine to it.'

The thin rider wagged his head.

'Dang animal leads like a mule, got a back of solid steel an' don't rein good.'

Morris was stepping back to the tie rack when he spoke to the thin man. 'Them kind is good for kids, friend.' He looked up at the bull-necked swarthy man. 'Much obliged.'

If Beckwourth might have replied he didn't get the chance. From over on the porch Timmy yelled. 'Four riders comin', Pa! I saw 'em weavin' in an' out of the trees!'

Morris looked northward, saw nothing and faced Hobart. 'Head for the house!'

As the pair of men on foot began to move quickly one of the rangemen called after them, 'What is it?'

Hobart answered over his shoulder. 'Renegade raiders!'

Beckwourth swung off, pulled his Winchester from its boot and yelled ahead. 'Hold up!' and told his companions to bring their weapons, forget their mounts and follow Hobart and Morris toward the house.

They obeyed without hesitation. Each of them was old enough to have either seen raiders or heard about them. The stories were grisly.

Hobart held the door aside until everyone was inside, then closed it. Beckwourth looked briefly around, saw the white-faced youth and stepped to the window as he spoke. 'First I've ever heard of renegades hereabouts, but this is the kind of place they'd raid for a fact, only a couple of men, too far for the sounds of gunfire to be heard.'

He turned, facing Alex Hobart, as the thin rangeman made a cackling laugh. When he finished he looked straight at Beckwourth. 'All because of that worthless damned buckskin.'

No one else saw the humour. Timmy disappeared beyond the kitchen and his father went after him. Hobart went to the door leading from the kitchen to the side porch, caught him in the doorway, swung him back into the room and took the lad's place. He stepped out on to the porch.

There were indeed four of them, and one was riding with a rifle across his lap, the other horsemen had booted carbines. They were moving through the last fringe of forest before reaching the clearing and they halted back there in shadowy gloom.

Alex Hobart poked his head back inside and said, 'Loaded for bear,' and continued to watch.

The riders were in no hurry and they were clearly being cautious. The last time they stopped was just clear of the forest where they sat gazing at the three saddled horses near the tie rack. They spoke among themselves. Alex could see them doing this but could not hear a word.

In sunlight, he recognized the town constable, the local blacksmith but not the other two.

As he went back inside and barred the door after himself, he caught Whit Morris's eye and jerked his head. The rangemen in the parlour were bunched by the window, they could see the distant horsemen and watched them.

Hobart spoke softly to Morris. 'It's that damned constable from town. The stocky feller directly behind him is the blacksmith.'

A rangeman called from the parlour window. 'Somethin's not right; renegades don't just set out there, they come at a dead run shootin' at everythin' in sight. If I had a rifle I could pick off that feller in front.'

Hobart and Morris returned to the parlour where Timmy was also at the window, he had his fragilelooking, old ball-and-powder rifle.

The rangeman who had said something was wrong asked Timmy if he could borrow his rifle. He said, 'I can part that son of a bitch's hair from here with that rifle, boy.'

Beckwourth saved Timmy from saying he would not hand over his grandpa's gun. Beckwourth said, 'I've heard they don't always come fast, surprise folks and kill everythin', Slim. Looks to me like they're settin' out there palaverin' about walkin' their horses up to the house like neighbours, or maybe like pilgrims that're lost.'

The thin rangeman was sceptical. 'Beck, how many times you seen a feller carryin' a rifle instead of a carbine?'

'Don't have to mean anythin', Slim.'

Timmy interrupted this exchange when he said, 'Here they come', and he was right. The four riders entered the yard at a walk and got as far as the barn when someone yelled to them.

They stopped, the lawman and blacksmith entered the barn and after an interval they returned to the yard with Dennis Grant between them.

He was massaging his arms as he glared in the direction of the house and spoke swiftly to Constable Drake.

8

Out and Back

Constable Drake stood clear and called toward the house. 'Hobart! Who's in there with you? Come out so's we can talk.'

The three rangemen turned to stare at Alex Hobart. Before they could speak, the lawman called again. 'You got Morris or whatever his name is, in there with you?'

The bull-necked swarthy man leaned his saddle gun aside. 'What in the hell is this about? Is your name Hobart?' When the pale-eyed, craggy man nodded, Beckwourth wagged his head. 'Mister, that's the law out there an' I don't take kindly to you for yellin' renegades . . . Mister, looks to me like we're forted up with the wrong people.'

Beckwourth's skinny companion went to a chair and sat down. The other rangeman grounded his Winchester impassively regarding Hobart and Morris.

Beckwourth spoke again. 'You cozened us to get in here with you, but if you figured we'd fight off a lawman and his posse riders . . . '

'*Hobart!* We're not goin' to stand out here all day,' Constable Drake yelled.

Whit Morris called back, 'You're out-numbered an' out-gunned. You want to come get us, come ahead!'

Henry Drake was neither a coward nor a fool. He crowded up his companions and they talked for a long time. The men inside watched. Beckwourth would not look at either Hobart or Morris.

It was Timmy, the old dog beside him, who broke the long silence. 'Pa, they're leavin'. Mister Drake's got Mister Grant ridin' double with him . . . Pa, why'd they leave Mister Grant's horse in the barn?'

Hobart didn't reply, that thin rangeman did. 'I don't know who they are but they wasn't dumb enough to take their guns an' go into the barn.'

As the dour lawman led his companions back toward the trees, Beckwourth turned on Alex Hobart. 'For a plugged *centavo* I'd stomp the whey out of you!'

Hobart looked straight back. 'Any time you're feelin' lucky,' he replied.

Morris drew and cocked his six-gun. No one who had ever heard a gun being cocked ignored it. Even Beckwourth looked around. Morris said, 'Much obliged for the help, gents, now get on your horses an' don't even think about comin' back. *Git*!'

They got; Beckwourth turned in the doorway and glared. Morris tipped the barrel of his handgun several inches and waited.

Beckwourth stamped out to the porch, down into the yard and joined his companions catching their animals, snugging up, swinging across leather

144

and riding out of the yard.

Morris eased down the dog, holstered his six-gun and looked at Alex Hobart. The older man sank down in a chair, looked at his son and said, 'You got to thank Mister Morris for buyin' you the buckskin horse.'

Timmy faced Morris, who raised a hand. 'Forget it, Tim. From what them rangemen said he's oak-stubborn and hard ridin'.'

Timmy leaned aside his grandfather's old gun and left the house with his old dog trailing him all the way to the barn, down through it to the corral. He climbed to the top stringer and told the buckskin he had a name. It would be Line-back; it was appropriate, there had never been a true buckskin born that wasn't line-backed.

Alex Hobart remained slumped in a chair until Morris said, 'I'd admire a go at the jug,' and the craggy, pale-eyed man arose to rummage in a small cabinet.

They both had a long pull after

which Hobart held the jug high and shook it. As he was putting it away, he said, 'Corn won't be ripe for another month or so but I'll get the still ready.'

Hobart was quiet a moment then burst into laughter. Morris stared, Hobart said, 'The look on that 'breed's face, the feller named Beckwourth,' and laughed again.

Morris didn't laugh. 'He'll have a story to tell his boss.'

Hobart gazed at Morris. 'How did that happen? Right when we didn't have a chance.'

Timmy had returned to the house and he now left the kitchen. He and his dog went out into the yard. Hobart made an accurate guess. 'Lad's finally got his own horse. He never come right out, but he's wanted one a long time.' Hobart gazed at Whit Morris. 'That was a right decent thing you did. Timmy'll never forget it.'

Morris was uncomfortable so he changed the subject. 'That Bullhead City lawman'll be back with reinforcements.'

Hobart's mood was clearly mellow. He made right powerful corn squeezings. 'Let him come. We'll be long gone.' Hobart arose. 'I'm tuckered. You . . . ?'

Morris arose nodding. He said, 'Got to be gone before sunrise.'

They parted. Morris went down to his storeroom and left the door open. Timmy appeared in the opening, clearing his throat. Morris glanced around, read the boy's expression right and held up a restraining hand. 'You said thanks. That's enough. You better go over yonder and bed down. We'll be cuttin' out early.'

The boy didn't move. 'Mister Morris?'

'Yes.'

'How'll it end?'

Morris eased down on an old bench that teetered. 'The Lord knows an' He won't say.' Morris paused and Timmy spoke again. 'There's too many an' they don't seem likely to let up.'

Morris nodded about that and made a small smile. 'We keep goin'. I think you'n your pa know the mountains better'n those flatlanders do.'

'That's what I mean, Mister Morris. We're goin' to fetch up like them hide-out In'ians, sneakin' around, do some night-ridin', livin' out of our hats.'

Morris considered Timmy. It did not require a whole lot of sense to guess about the lad's future. Morris said, 'Timmy, life's not always fair. In our fix now I'd guess we got to make some hard decisions or give up.'

'We can't give up, Mister Morris. They'll hang my pa.'

Morris agreed, but not out loud. He asked a question. 'Then what do we do?'

Timmy's expression was more upset than tired, but he had to be tired. Youth was resilient but even the young had limits.

As he was turning away he said, 'Keep runnin' I guess,' and left the doorway on his way across to the house.

Morris did not leave the rickety

148

bench for a while. He searched for answers, found none and bedded down. How he had got into this mess was anyone's guess but for a blessed fact he was in it up to his neck.

Shortly before falling asleep he smiled. Alex Hobart's laughter echoed in his mind. For a fact those rangemen had come in right handy.

He probably wouldn't have awakened as early as he did but for a large rat running blind in darkness which ran across his chest and squeaked.

He waved his hat but the rat was long gone. He sat up, groped for his boots and had dropped his hat on when Alex Hobart appeared in the doorway. He was bundled into an old blanket coat and was carrying his saddle gun. They nodded without speaking and Hobart went in the direction of the barn.

From habit, Whit Morris functioned best after hot coffee in the morning but there wouldn't be time. He left the

149

storeroom door ajar and also headed for the barn.

Timmy was rigging out his buckskin. He too nodded without speaking.

As they left the yard in darkness, Morris noticed the croaker sacks made fast behind Alex Hobart's saddle. The would-be presidential assassin was someone who believed in being prepared.

It was cold and remained so even after sunrise. In open country the world would be warming up, not in the timbered highlands where sunlight rarely shone past interwoven tree limbs.

They didn't make a sound but that was incidental; for a while being silent wouldn't matter.

Hobart clearly had a destination. All Morris understood was that it would be north-easterly. Hobart only changed course where dense timber required it and he afterwards returned to his route.

Morris wasn't very concerned. If they had to hide out for a year or more he was satisfied that flatland posse riders would not find them. Not even with an Indian tracker.

When heat eventually arrived the day was half spent. They stopped at a watercourse to tank up the horses and themselves and here for the first time since they left the homestead Alex Hobart spoke. He did this as he removed his coat and leaned to make it fast behind the cantle.

'There's an old couple got a homestead near Brandon. It'll take us two, three days to get there. They knew me'n my wife in Alabama. They lost a son in the war. I stumbled on to 'em years back'n now an' then, when I'm over that way, I stop an' visit.'

Morris found a deadfall and sat on it watching the pale-eyed craggy older man. 'That's where we're goin'?'

'Yes. To stop over.'

'Where'll we go after that?'

Hobart faced around. Both Morris and his son looked steadily at him. Hobart said, 'I don't exactly know.'

Morris said, 'There's settlements, the telegraph, roads an' people. The farther east we go the worse it'll be for fugitives.'

Hobart let go a long sigh. Before he could speak his son said, 'Pa, what about Shep?'

Hobart sank down in a bare place. 'Timmy, we got to get so far off we'll be safe. If they catch us . . . '

'Pa, Shep's old and stove up. He can't make it on his own.'

Hobart looked from his son to the gloomily shadowed easterly forest.

Morris finally spoke. 'We're goin' to ride our butts sore headin' into settlement country, Alex.'

Hobart sat slumped. He did not raise his head when he said, 'I'm tired, Whit. I'm about wore out from bein' hunted.'

Morris eyed the older man. Hobart was beaten; among frontiersmen he was what was called 'spirit broken'.

While Hobart went for the sacks behind his saddle so they could eat

Morris made a decision he did not like, but he liked even less riding aimlessly in settled country. He said nothing until Alex handed each of them food, then he said, 'Alex, I dassn't do it. When we get among settled folks we'll be strangers, pretty rough-lookin' strangers. Folks ask questions . . . I'm goin' west. If you got to give up, I can't do it.'

None of them ate very much, Timmy least of all. What little in his world he had come to rely upon, was falling apart. He jumped up and went out where his buckskin was cropping grass, leaned with both arms over the horse's back and lowered his head.

Both men saw him out there. Morris was building a smoke when he said, 'When somethin' happens to you, Alex, the boy'll have nothin'. I've seen cast-off kids on their own. Mostly, they don't make it.'

Hobart methodically put things back into one of the croaker sacks. When he faced back toward Morris he had the expression of someone suffering acute stomach complaint. 'You could take the lad, Whit.'

Morris's eyes widened. For a long time he was silent. He'd had no idea the older man would make such a statement. Later, he would wonder if Hobart hadn't had that in mind during the silent long miles they had been riding.

Indignation arose in Morris. 'What in hell . . . Alex, you're all that boy's got.'

'Sooner or later they'll get me, Whit. Don't you think I know that? Then what'll happen to him?'

Morris's exasperation made his voice rise as he said, 'You gawdamned idiot. If it was just you we'd part company here an' now. If you didn't have the boy I'd say go ahead an' get yourself hung. But you ain't alone, for Chris'sake. Keep on ridin' easterly an' sure, they'll nail you sooner or later. If they're mean folks they'll make Timmy watch his pa get hung.' His voice softened but it was hard. 'Last night when he come by to thank me again for the damned horse I got to thinkin'. He's young but he's got a limit, the same kind you're showin' right now. Alex, answer me a question: what would your wife think?'

Hobart sat slumped and silent. When Timmy returned with high colour and moist eyes his father looked up, arose and said, 'Let's ride,' and went to get his mount. Timmy watched briefly then faced Whit Morris, who also arose but ignored the boy to go after his animal.

When they were ready to mount with Timmy watching them both, his father swung astride, reined around and headed back the way they had come.

Timmy waited until his father was too far ahead to hear then asked Morris why they were going back. Morris's answer was cryptic. 'He knows the country back yonder.'

Timmy had to be satisfied with that.

The next time they halted was in the

clearing where Morris had first stopped and set up camp. Devil's Den.

They were not far from the homestead. Hobart and Whit Morris did not speak to each other but Timmy did not notice this.

The following morning they left Devil's Den travelling westerly. Alex angled northerly until they were in higher country from which they could see the log house and its adjoining clearings.

Timmy mentioned his dog and the other animals. They would need caring for. His father sat his horse with tight lips wearing an expression that defied defining. Whit Morris had a hunch. If Hobart headed for his cabin . . . by now there'd be possemen behind every blessed tree and rock.

Someone made a sound of rocks being disturbed and rolling together. It was a distant sound but audible. Morris picked up his reins. The worst that could happen to him was prison, but he'd be alive. He watched Alex like a hawk. If he reined southward where as sure as Gawd made sour apples there was an ambush waiting, Morris was going to climb higher and ride due west.

Hobart softly said, 'They're down there, Whit.'

Morris didn't reply; obviously they were down there.

A dog barked once, then gave a yelp of pain when someone hit it. Timmy broke away in a zigzag lope. His father raised his rein hand but did not move. Morris swore under his breath before saying, 'Alex, sure as we're settin' here when he comes chargin' out of the trees some trigger-happy son of a bitch will shoot him.'

If Morris hadn't said that he and Hobart might have sat there, but Alex Hobart spun his mount, hooked it hard and went zigzagging in a lope after his son.

Morris sat a moment before saying aloud, 'Mister Gawd, it's up to You,' and went charging in Hobart's tracks.

He could eventually make out the buckskin horse in the yard, standing like a stone without a rider on its back. If there had been a gunshot Morris had not heard it; maybe a bushwhacker had knocked Timmy off his horse with a club. Maybe a lot of things; the lad was not in sight but the buckskin horse was.

The day was nearly spent; in another hour or such a matter, dusk would settle. Until it did Alex Hobart's run toward the yard made two good targets, Alex and his horse.

Morris was down where stumps allowed dying daylight to show the house and clearings. He yanked loose the six-gun's tie-down thong, drew the gun and held it in his right hand ready but not cocked.

Hobart left his horse near the barn, carbine in hand. There was no sign of Tommy. Hobart was half crouched and tense. The only sound was of Morris coming in a lope. Hobart saw the oncoming rider, knew who he was and remained crouched and ready with the carbine in both hands.

Morris was not and never had been a praying man. He didn't even believe very strongly in luck. If he'd had time he would have cursed himself for what he was doing but that wouldn't, couldn't stop him from doing it.

He cleared the last of the stumps and timber, sixgun riding high, thumb pad on the hammer when sunlight hit him. He was unaware of anything but the bewildered buckskin and Alex Hobart in front of his barn crouched and ready.

Morris cleared the last shadow and raised his left hand slightly to slacken the rush of his horse. Something was wrong.

There were no gunshots. Except for the fact that Timmy was not in sight the yard was empty but for Timmy's father and two baffled horses, Hobart's animal and the buckskin.

9

Good Odds

Morris left his animal on the fly, lit running and went into some late-day shadows north of the barn. There was not a sound but for the three horses shifting their feet. Alex Hobart eventually straightened out of his crouch a little, Morris squinted for a hostile sighting and saw nothing, whoever they were and how ever many of them there were, they were as quiet as clouds.

Hobart finally called his son's name. The only response was an echo. Morris heard the cooped quail make their little chuckling sound. They were probably hungry. Moments passed. That big red rooster appeared, head-up proud, herding five or six hens who completely ignored his best handsome effort to make himself appealing.

Morris, six-gun balanced shoulder high, began to get less tense and anxious and more mystified and annoyed. He called once, 'Stand up! Constable Drake if you're out there there's just the two of us. You want a fight we'll give you one!'

There was still no answer but movement around the south side of the barn caught and held Morris's attention. He couldn't see around there but in the silence he had no difficulty hearing sounds of someone walking.

Hobart's back was to the barn. He too heard sounds along the far side of his barn and twisted from the waist.

Morris shook his head. He had to assume Hobart's stance in front of his barn was prompted by anxiety about his son, but it was a poor place to stand if there was anyone behind him in the barn which Morris felt certain there would be.

A man called into the stillness. 'Hobart, I got your boy. You hear me?'

The answer came swiftly and harshly. 'You hurt him an' I'll spend the rest of my life makin' you wish you'd never been born!'

The voice from the south side of the barn was without inflection when it said, 'Where's the other three fellers, sneakin' around in the trees?'

For a moment Hobart didn't answer. When he finally did answer he made a challenge. 'Turn my boy loose an' maybe they won't blow your head off. *Turn him loose*!'

The answer came in the same inflectionless tone. 'We're comin' around in front. Me'n your boy. You look like you're goin' to shoot an' you better think hard because the boy'll be in front of me.'

Morris leaned as far as he dared without leaving the shadows, watched the far corner of the barn and when two figures emerged he recognized them both: Timmy and Town Constable Drake. The lawman had one arm around Timmy's neck. They stopped

162

where Hobart could see them and Constable Drake said, 'There wasn't no other way, Mister Hobart. There are seven possemen hid out watchin'. Where are them fellers who forted-up with you yestiddy?'

'They're gone. Tim, you all right?'

The boy nodded. The arm across his throat made talking difficult but he said, 'I'm all right. I got knocked off my horse is all. Pa . . . '

'Set him loose,' Hobart said. 'Drake, I'll break your gawdamned neck! *Turn him loose!*'

Morris didn't have a clear sighting but he lowered his six-gun.

The constable loosened his hold and Timmy leaned forward a little. Drake said, 'The reason I come up here is to talk to you.'

Hobart sneered. 'So you brought along an army.'

'Yestiddy when you forted-up in the house I wasn't goin' to take the risk.'

'You puss-gutted, miserable son . . . '

'Listen to me, damn it. Shut up and

listen.' As Drake said this he released Timmy and gave him a slight shove in his father's direction.

'Mister Hobart, I got to tell you, gettin' to talk to you is worth a man's life. I got a copy of a letter that concerns you. I got it in my pocket, you goin' to shoot me when I reach for it?'

Hobart did not respond, Constable Drake moved his left hand very slowly toward his hip pocket and moved it just as slowly as he brought it forward holding a folded and rumpled envelope.

He held it out without speaking. Alex told his son to take the envelope, which Timmy did, and handed it to his father.

One of the horses shoved out a foreleg and clicked its teeth as it bit a bug bite. That was the only sound as Alex Hobart read and reread the letter.

He handed the saddle gun to Timmy, went back to lean on the tie rack and read the letter very slowly for the third time.

Constable Drake broke the silence. 'That's all I was tryin' to do, give you that damned letter, but every time I come close you . . . '

Morris leathered his weapons and walked over to the tie rack where Alex was leaning with the letter dangling from one hand. He took the letter, read it, jerked his chin for Timmy to come close and handed him the letter. Timmy's father was limply leaning staring at nothing.

Morris addressed the lawman. 'Who opened it?'

'Me. Well . . . '

'It had his name on the envelope.'

Drake reddened. 'He was a wanted man. You got to understand where I stood. He stole a cow an' . . . '

Someone called from the east side of the yard where he had been concealed. 'Henry, it's hot an' gettin' late.'

Several men appeared, two from inside the barn. Morris watched them emerge behind Hobart at the tie rack and shook his head for the second time.

Constable Drake repeated an earlier question. 'Them fellers who was in the cabin with you . . . who was they?'

Morris answered because Alex Hobart was crossing slowly toward the house beside his son. The old dog came from beneath the porch and cringed. Timmy stopped and turned. 'Which one of you hit my dog?' he called to the possemen assembling around the town constable. The blacksmith faced around. 'I did. The damned mutt tried to bite me.'

Timmy walked back without taking his eyes off the burly balding man, stopped and kicked. As the blacksmith doubled over in agony one of the other possemen started for Timmy. He stopped to look over his shoulder when Morris cocked his six-gun.

The blacksmith was in real agony, when the others went to fetch their hidden saddle animals the blacksmith remained doubled over, his face twisted in pain.

Constable Drake leaned to help the blacksmith straighten up and got knocked aside.

Morris went close to the blacksmith and said, 'If it'd been my dog I'd of gut shot you.' Morris faced the town constable. 'Get out of here. For a plugged *centavo* I'd beat the whey out of you. *Get astride and get away from here and stay away!*'

Constable Drake started to speak. Morris stepped close and punched the lawman in the chest with a stiff finger. 'Don't open your gawdamned mouth. Get on your horse and don't even look back.'

Several possemen looked hard at Morris. He showed them a death's-head grin. They swung astride and headed out of the yard. Constable Drake didn't lead, he brought up the rear. His posse riders were tired, hungry and disgusted. In the opinion of several of them Drake had handled everything wrong.

After the last man left, Morris collected the riderless animals, off-saddled and bridled them, led them out back to the corral and turned them in.

There was an extra horse. He ignored that, pitched hay and headed for the house.

Alex was sprawled in a chair on the porch looking far out. Timmy was talking to someone in the kitchen who didn't answer.

Morris pulled a chair around, sat and said, 'Who the hell is Rutherford Hayes?' and got a mumbled answer. 'President of the country.' The sound of his own voice may have coaxed Alex out of his reverie. 'Why did they have to wait so damned long?'

Morris offered no answer because he had none, but if he had known more he might have said Alex Hobart's pardon had to take that long, trying to assassinate a president couldn't have been pardoned any earlier. Hobart was fortunate, other similar attempts at

168

assassination had been dealt with more harshly.

Close to twenty years had passed, almost a whole generation. Whoever had instituted the pardon probably thought enough time had passed.

Hobart remained on the porch when Timmy called them to eat. Morris went inside. Timmy raised his eyebrows and Morris simply shook his head.

Neither of them could understand. In a way, the executive pardon piled one burden after another on the craggy man sitting in the lowering night only someone in his situation could understand.

Morris passed the still figure on the porch on his way to the storeroom where he discovered that leaving the door open to mitigate odours hadn't been the best idea he'd ever had. It wasn't rats this time, it was three large grey squirrels gnawing on his saddle blanket because it was permeated with salt from horse sweat.

He aimed a wild kick at them and

one squirrel leapt almost in his face in its attempt to flee. After they were gone Morris closed the door, examined his saddle blanket by candlelight and groaned. As he rolled and lighted a smoke he remembered something he'd once heard one of those itinerant preachers say: Into every life a little rain must fall.

It had sounded poetic when the preacher had said it. For two bits if he had the preacher in front of him in the storeroom he'd have been tempted to make him eat those words.

In the morning, with the sun barely over the far curve of the world, Morris rolled his blankets, went down to catch his horse and saddle up. Timmy called from the house, breakfast was ready.

Morris smiled. If Timmy had been a girl it wouldn't have been unusual, girls cooked, boys didn't.

Alex was waiting when Whit entered the cabin. He had seen Morris lead his horse into the barn to be rigged out. He was in the middle of the parlour holding a cup of coffee when he said, 'You goin' ridin'?'

Morris nodded. 'It's settled. You're pardoned. Timmy's got a horse. I'll head out.'

'You could stay,' the craggy-faced man softly said.

Morris smiled. 'No; you'n Timmy are settled in.'

'Where will you go?'

'I woke up ponderin' about goin' over to Devil's Den. Maybe find out if it's homestead land an' file on it.'

Hobart's solemn gaze brightened a little. 'I know about homesteadin'; I can ride down yonder an' help you file the papers.'

Timmy appeared in the kitchen doorway. 'It's gettin' cold,' he said. The older men filed into the kitchen, sat down and ate. Timmy talked; the men at the table either were silent or answered indifferently.

After breakfast, with the sun full up, they left Timmy in the kitchen, walked down to the barn and Alex brought up their previous subject. 'Homesteadin' isn't hard. To qualify you got to build a house with at least one window, agree to stay on the land three years to prove up, then you get your deed.'

Morris listened and when he was ready to lead his horse outside to be mounted he said, 'You'd have a neighbour,' and Hobart smiled. 'It'd suit me.'

'You told me once you wanted to be left alone.'

'I did, an' I suppose I still do, but Devil's Den's far enough so's we wouldn't bother each other.' Hobart paused. 'You want me to ride down yonder an' help you file on the mesa?'

Morris was still and silent for a time then looped the reins and faced around. 'I'd be plumb grateful. Today?'

'Right now. I'll tell Timmy we'll be gone a spell.'

Morris had the barn to himself after Alex Hobart returned to the house. He pondered. He had never owned land, had never 'settled in' anywhere for long. Devil's Den . . . a wandering man couldn't find a better place; a long ride from the town, high enough for a man to see riders coming before they got close. He'd never be pardoned the way Alex had been, but he'd be about as safely secluded as a man could be and still have some grassland as well as miles of primitive country at his back if he had to use it.

When Alex returned, he said Timmy would have supper ready when they got back and went to bring in his animal and saddle up.

The sun was well above the horizon, heat was building except in the timber, but they skirted easterly on a downhill angle until they reached grassland, then headed directly for the village with two windmills.

Entering Bullhead City from the north made both men straighten up in their saddles. They saw two men who had been with the constable. They nodded and one of the townsmen nodded back.

Down at the livery barn where they handed over their horses to the elfin proprietor he hardly spoke.

The land office was in a spot between the harness works and an apothecary's store.

The clerk wore a pale-green shirt with fluffy sleeve garters. He was business-like and when Alex Hobart explained their reason for being in his office, the man opened a desk drawer, removed several printed papers and handed them to Whit Morris. 'Fill 'em out as best you can. Dates ought to close. If you need help I'll be handy.'

They took the papers over to the saloon, sat at a round poker table, called for beer and a pencil which the barman provided without looking the least curious, and went to work on the application form.

Where the applicant's name was required Morris raised his head. Hobart said, 'Whitman Morris,' and paused before saying the rest of it. 'That's who you'll be from here on. Whatever

174

you was before was someone else.'

Morris filled out the paper, sat back while Alex Hobart read it, and Constable Drake came in, crossed to the table and waited to be seen.

Morris kicked a chair around. 'Set, Mister Drake. I'm filin' homestead rights on that mesa up yonder. The one folks call Devil's Den.'

The man who never smiled lightly scratched his nose before saying, 'You heard about the haunts up there?'

Morris nodded.

The lawman leaned on the table considering his large hands. 'Well, I never put no store in that crap, but the Messicans do, an' some *gringos* do too.'

Hobart handed the paper back to Morris. He and the town constable exchanged an expressionless gaze without speaking until Henry Drake said, 'Mister, I got to thinkin' yestiddy. Why didn't they do that ten, twelve years back?'

Hobart did not answer, he instead

asked a question of his own. 'All the years I lived up yonder, you didn't know there was a bounty out on me?'

'All's I knew, Mister Hobart, was that you set up in a place pretty well apart an' that you seldom come to town. Sure, I wondered. You wouldn't be the first feller who hid out, but I never seen a dodger on you; you never made no trouble until you stole that damned cow.'

Morris listened, studied the town constable and made his judgement, which was correct: Henry Drake was one of those people who did nothing he wasn't driven to do. He was big, soured on life and lazy. If folks went out of their way to hire a lawman who holed up in his jailhouse in winter and did the same during hot summers, they couldn't have found a better man.

One thing troubled him about the phlegmatic town constable, so he said, 'Why 'd you stand by when that son of a bitch whaled hell out of Alex's boy?'

'He jumped the lad before I could get up an' stop him. It was over about that fast too.'

'An' you wouldn't let no one look after the boy?'

Constable Drake got a pained look on his face. 'Mister, if it got known there'd have been hell to pay. The boy wasn't hurt bad an' my job's to keep things peaceful an' quiet.' Drake paused. 'What the boy's pa done to Dennis squared it up, an' what the boy done to the blacksmith settled that score too. In case you want to know, the blacksmith still can't straighten up real good . . . mister, that's no way for folks to fight.'

Morris made a wolfish smile. 'That blacksmith would have beat him until he couldn't stand alone.'

'But that's no place to kick a man.'

Morris gazed at the town constable without speaking. Across from him Alex Hobart kicked back his chair and arose. He hadn't taken part in the discussion between the other two men, but now he did. He leaned, looking steadily into the lawman's face. 'You tell that blacksmith the next time he comes on to my claim, I'll bury the son of a bitch. An' that goes for the feller named Grant.'

They left the lawman sitting as they left the saloon to return to the land office.

There would be a delay, the land agent told them. A search had to be made before the application could be approved, in case someone else had filed on the same land. He also asked for ten dollars for the filing fee.

As Morris counted out the money he asked how long it would take before his application would be granted.

As the clerk counted the greenbacks he answered in an offhand manner. 'In your case, mister, I'd say no more'n a month. It usually takes three, four months.' The clerk put the filing fee in a drawer and raised his eyes to Morris. 'I can tell you for a fact no one's filed on that hunnert an' sixty.' He made a tight small smile. 'If the government was givin' land away no one from around here would file on that piece. It's haunted. Story is there was a massacre up there years back an' ghosts mock folks as go up there.'

They left the land agent's office, went over to the café run by the sullen-eyed woman, were the only customers and gave their orders. The woman would not look directly at either of them.

After they had eaten and put coins beside the empty plates the women appeared from her cooking area. She was youngish and attractive. She wore no wedding ring for an excellent reason, over the years she had learned to heartily dislike men. As she scooped up the coins she ignored Morris and addressed Alex Hobart. 'I've seen you before once or twice. There's a story going around . . . did you really try to assassinate Gen'l Grant?'

Alex stood looking at the younger woman, expressionless and cold-eyed. 'Lady, the way I was raised, folks never asked personal questions.'

The woman was not offended or, if she was she didn't show it. She said, 'Too bad you missed. My pa an' uncle died, one in a Yankee prison camp, the other with Gen'ral Stuart's cavalry in Virginia.'

Alex Hobart did not unbend. 'That was long ago. It don't do no good keepin' it alive.'

Her answer was short. 'It's too bad you missed. Any time you're in town come by; I feed old Rebels for nothin'.'

When they were outside, Hobart put a pained look on Whit Morris. 'It'll never leave me, will it?'

Morris led off for their animals as he dryly replied, 'I would resent bein' called an old Rebel less than I'd like bein' called just a Rebel . . . She's pretty, did you notice?'

Hobart walked along looking and feeling indignant. 'No, I didn't notice.'

When they were halfway toward the highlands Hobart's mood changed. 'Timmy an' I'll help you cut logs an' haul them. The three of us could get your house up before winter. You doin' it alone . . . you'd never make it.'

Morris left Hobart on his mesa. He had some gatherings to be retrieved from the Hobart place which he would go after in a day or two. Right now he wanted to go over where the creek was, where the burned stones of his fire ring were, hobble the horse, sit on his own land and just have a smoke.

He'd never owned land before, although he'd often thought that someday he would. A man didn't have to have a family to have a homing instinct.

When night came he rassled a meal of scraps from his saddle-bags, mostly dry jerky, and spread the bedroll from behind his saddle, and looked straight up.

181

If there was life up there, two-legged life, which he thought there surely had to be among those millions of stars, he wondered if there wasn't maybe another rider who was fixing to settle in.

10

First Blood

It helped that the days were long and warm; downing fir trees and snaking them to the place Morris wanted his house, near the creek where his fire ring was, and draw-knifing them took time. It also helped that they had horses to drag the timber; Morris didn't want to take down the nearest ones to his mesa.

Timmy was tireless, the older men were not. If they had been it probably wouldn't have taken as long as it did to get four walls up and dowel in the fir rafters.

They had no interference for three weeks, and even then while it was something to think about, it did not appear menacing: shod-horse tracks which appeared to originate somewhere south-westerly meandered around Devil's Den within the shielding fringe of big trees. Alex said they had been curious people, perhaps townsmen. Morris asked why, then, if they'd been curious and interested they hadn't come into the open where they would have been welcome.

Alex, who had been sharpening and oiling the teeth of a cross-cut saw allowed the matter to drop. In order to file saw teeth to the precise angle required concentration, and for several days the prowlers or whatever they were, did not leave fresh tracks, something which seemed to substantiate Alex's end of the conversation.

On an overcast day they were able to cinch the draw-knifed fir rafters. When the sun returned they sat on fir rounds splitting sugar pine squares into shakes for the roof.

Most settlers did not know the difference and roofed their buildings with yellow pine shingles, but they would learn that although pine was easier to split to size, it did not stand up under harsh weather as well as fir shingles did.

There was a framed-in door facing southward and a cut-out in the west wall for a window. One evening as they dined at the fire ring, Alex heaved a great sigh. By the light of a dying day he studied the cabin and was satisfied. 'Few more days,' he said, and abruptly asked a question. 'What do you figure to make that window out of?'

Morris said, 'They got glass ones at the store down yonder.'

Hobart wagged his head. 'One of them storebought glass windows'll cost you more'n the house cost. Next deer you kill an' skin, scrape the hide until it's real thin. You can't see out very good but them windows won't cost anythin' an' they let sunlight through.'

Morris said nothing. He wanted a glass window. He rolled a smoke and winked at Timmy. 'How're you'n the line-back horse gettin' along?'

If he had known he was opening a

Pandora's box he never would have asked. Timmy's horse was almost as close to him as the old dog, who accompanied them every day over to the mesa and went home with them after daylight faded.

'I call him Chief now an' he ain't hard to lead. He's been struck in the face so he hangs back. I got him to lead good an' foller me'n Shep. He's a good horse. Some don't like to be rode bareback; he don't care at all. He reins like a cuttin' horse, comes up in front and wheels on his back legs. I wouldn't take a million dollars for him.'

Morris and Alex exchanged a look. Alex made a slight wag of his head.

'I've rode him just about everywhere. He's gettin' tender in front.' Timmy paused looking at Whit Morris. 'You know how to shoe, Mister Morris?'

This time the boy's father spoke up. 'We don't have no shoes, Timmy. An' a man needs a forge an' an anvil.'

Morris watched the youth nod and scratched his head. He said, 'I'll pick up some shoes next time I go down yonder. Anvil? For a fact a man needs one, but I've warped shoes over boulders an' got 'em hot in a brush fire.'

Timmy was placated. His father sent him to bring in the saddle animals and when he was gone Alex said, 'Whit, don't spoil the boy. Bein' raised hard'll fit him for life.'

Morris said nothing. When the Hobarts were rigged out for the ride home and as they were passing into timber, Alex said something to his son and no answer came over as far as where Morris was sitting.

He got up and despite decreasing visibility went hunting for an echo box in the vicinity the Hobarts had ridden past.

He found it, but by accident. Usually echo boxes were concealed. This one had been brushed clear on top. Morris took it back by the fire and examined it. It was crudely made, had three sides and a top. Inside on the back wall was some kind of metal.

He put it aside, washed at the creek and took his soogans inside the house to sleep on the earthen floor. He could see past rafters where stars shone, smiled and slept the only way someone whose day had been spent at hard labour would sleep.

In the morning he was crouching near the fire ring having a smoke after eating when Alex, Timmy and Shep came out of the timber more northerly than they usually did.

They rode up, dismounted and after Alex handed his reins to the boy he took Whit Morris inside and said, 'More shod-horse tracks, Whit. Three sets. Pardner, they're not nosy flatlanders, they stopped a couple of places where they had a good sightin' of the mesa. Whoever they are they're interested in what we're doin' an' I'd guess they got a camp some-where about. They wouldn't be lawmen, not the way they skulk around. I think maybe Timmy'n I better sleep over here for a spell.'

Morris accepted the suggestion with

a nod. Lately he'd begun to ignore subtle noises and shadows. However, as Alex had said, if they were lawmen they'd simply ride out, throw down on him and make an arrest.

There wasn't much said as they sat in shade splitting fir shakes for the roof. Once Shep got his hackles up and growled while looking north-westerly. The shake-makers ignored the dog but as Hobart worked, he quietly said, 'Gettin' up their nerve. You want to trap 'em?'

'How?'

'Me'n Timmy'll saddle up an' head for home like we done every evenin' for the last month or so, then we'll go south an' watch.'

Whit said, 'It might be a long watch, Alex.'

Hobart was positioning his axe for a strike with the maul when he replied. 'Might be for a fact.' He made the split and moved his hand axe for the next strike. 'I believe they're up to no good, Whit.'

They sent Timmy up the pole ladder and handed up roofing shakes, until he had a couple of squares in place and had to straddle rafters. He had an advantage, not only was he lighter than the men but he could swing around up there like a monkey.

The overcast which had lingered for several days drifted in the direction of open country. When the sun returned it did so with a vengeance. Even in shade men sweated. Out on the graze the animals minded heat less, exactly as later they would mind the cold less.

When it appeared they had an adequate pile of shakes they left Timmy up above to secure them in place, which wasn't a difficult job although it was exacting. Each tier had to be aligned and each shake had to overlap the lower tier.

Morris wondered if they were being watched and when Alex gravely inclined his head Morris said, 'Let's go roust 'em.'

This time Alex shook his head, led

the way inside the house and said, 'Pretty big odds, Whit, an' us walkin' across the clearin' toward 'em could get us both shot.'

With a lowering sun and increasing shadows, they quit for the day, cleaned up at the creek, did everything they had been routinely doing for weeks, even made a cooking fire, ate, and although there was less said than at other evenings, when Alex and his boy were ready to depart and while Timmy was bringing in the horses, Alex told Whit Morris it might be wise if he stayed inside. There was no way of telling who the stalkers were or what they had in mind, but four stout log walls would be excellent protection if Morris needed it. Alex also said, 'They done their scoutin'-up. They know how we do things. Maybe it won't be tonight, maybe it'll be tomorrow night or the next one . . . ' Alex shrugged, turned to rig out with his son and ride the way they had been riding to and from Devil's Den for weeks.

Whit Morris went inside the house, made sure his belt-gun and carbine were fully loaded, rolled a smoke and while looking upward could no longer see the entire star-bright panorama. Timmy had shingled over a goodly section of the roof.

He went to stand in the doorway and watched his horse. Horses lacked a lot of being as good as dogs at rousing folks but he had no dog so he watched the horse.

In high, timbered country, darkness followed dusk without an interval. There was a moon, half a moon anyway.

Morris went to his bedroll near the stone ring and stuffed it with swatches of grass. The lumps were pretty much in the right places. It wouldn't fool anyone in daylight but it might fool them after moonrise.

He dozed, had to make a real effort to stay awake. There was nothing like manual labour to make a man dog-tired after day's end.

An owl hooted. Morris waited for an answer. When it came the second owl was a considerable distance in the timber. If there hadn't been an answer Morris would have had no trouble remaining awake.

To pass time, he made a mental list of things he'd need from the store in Bullhead City. After that he went around examining how the logs fitted from inside the cabin.

There would be considerable chinking to do, even adzing the bottoms of logs to make a flat fit top and bottom did not eliminate all the places where wind could come through.

It was while he was feeling along the east wall that he heard what could have been a night critter except that the width of its steps was too wide.

He edged along the south wall belt-gun in hand. An easily distinguished voice said, 'Find a club. Brain the bastard so's when he wakes up it'll be real hot.'

The second voice Morris recognized,

he had heard it when it was calm and when it was agitated: Beckwourth. It spoke sharply, 'Wait, Mike.'

'Why?'

'Come closer. He ain't in there, it's stuffed to look like he is.'

There was another sound.

Morris inched his way toward the doorless opening. When he was close enough he cocked the handgun and if it had been quiet before it now became utterly still until someone ripped out a curse and ran down the east wall. If there had been a window . . . but there wasn't.

Morris took down a big breath and poked his head out to see. The bedroll was where he had left it but there was no one nearby.

He inched out a little more. If they were out there they had probably followed in the wake of the man who had fled.

He moved along the east side of the house. He would be able to see the nearest trees from the northeast corner.

There was nothing moving. Except for his horse standing out yonder like a statue, little ears pointing in the direction the night-raiders had fled there was no visible evidence that they had been there.

Morris went back inside, leathered his sidearm and made a smoke. Alex was right. It helped to be able to identify one of them and it only required a moment to guess about the bull-necked man's companions. While in the Hobart yard one of them had said they would be paid off, as happened with all seasonal rangemen.

It took Morris longer to guess why they had been stalking him. He had paid a fistful of greenbacks for the line-backed horse and out-of-work rangemen just naturally sought another source of income. They figured Morris had money which was a pretty good guess.

They did not return. When Alex and Timmy appeared Alex had a carbine booted under the right *rosadero* of his saddle.

When Whit related his experience the previous night while Timmy was taking horses out to be hobbled, his father looked long in the direction of the northerly forest as he said, 'That'll leave 'em with two choices, won't it? Ride on an' forget raidin' you, or get up enough Dutch courage to try again.'

They sat in shade where the shingle blocks were. It put them in sight of anyone watching from the timber.

Alex worked methodically, said very little and when it was time for Timmy to go up the pole ladder, Alex gathered up two bundles of shakes and went over to hand them up.

A single gunshot blew apart the stillness and Alex dropped like a stone. Morris emptied his six-gun in the direction from which the shot had come. There was neither noise nor movement which meant the shooter had probably been behind a forest giant when he fired. His companions might have also got behind trees. If they hadn't, if they had run to get clear, there would have been movement. There had been no movement.

Timmy ran to his father. Morris went over there too, hunkered and reloaded his six-gun while Timmy was pawing his father and speaking in a quavering voice.

Alex sat up, dusted dirt and shavings off and twisted to consider his torn shirt and a thin trickle of blood. The bullet had grazed his ribs.

They went inside where Alex tore a shirttail to bandage his injury. His only comment was a growl. 'Couldn't hit the side of a barn from the inside.'

Morris went to the only window hole, which was in the west wall, stood well to one side and looked over where forest gloom prevented sunlight from penetrating. There was nothing to see. If there had been gun smoke it had dissipated.

Timmy would have gone outside but

his father growled and he came back. He was badly upset. He told his father he wished he had his grandfather's old muzzle-loader and Alex nodded without commenting.

Timmy replaced Morris at the window hole; when Whit moved toward the door he too got growled at by Alex. 'One target today is enough . . . wish I'd brought the jug along.'

Morris started to speak when Timmy called out and raised a rigid arm. Both older men went over there.

A man was crawling through high grass toward the horses. Alex went back for his carbine as he said, 'He's not goin' to set us afoot if I can help it.'

Morris lost sight of the crawling man when he veered to keep the horses between himself and the cabin.

Alex stood to one side of the opening and peeked around. Timmy's buckskin horse was edging away from something in the grass. The buckskin was between the house and the crawling man.

Morris said, 'Hell!' and went to the

198

doorway which provided an angling view. He raised his carbine, took a hand rest on the nearest log and fired.

Immediately two other guns fired toward the house and Morris had to duck back.

Alex fired three times as fast as he could lever up and fire. No one fired back. Alex grounded his Winchester and said, 'Short of a stick of dynamite they can't get us out of here, an' them damned trees is on their side.'

Timmy cried out again. The man Morris would have sworn he had hit crawling toward the horses was running as fast as he could. He made it to the timber before he could be fired at.

Morris said, 'I don't believe it. I never missed like that in my life.'

Alex provided a plausible answer. 'When he was crawlin' out there he was pushin' a carbine ahead. If he was doin' the same when you fired you maybe shot where him pushin' the carbine ahead made the grass shake.'

Alex told Timmy to stay clear of the

window. As he said this he and Morris were reloading.

There were no more gunshots toward the cabin. The afternoon wore along. Hobart told Morris he and Timmy had better stay the night at the house; riding back through the forest could get them both shot.

Morris agreed by nodding his head as he twisted to consider the older man's injury, it was still trickling blood. Hobart adjusted his shirttail bandage to take care of that. It wasn't the wound that hurt, it hadn't felt any worse than a bee sting, but a couple of his ribs were painful.

11

Fight!

In after times, Whit Morris would reflect on the stupidity of his raiders. All they would have had to do was wait out the Hobarts then attack him alone.

As someone had once said, it was a mistake to attribute intelligence to violent people.

Timmy remained high strung and tense. He alternately went from the hole in the wall to the doorless opening and although he did not expose himself his father watched and wagged his head.

The sun passed overhead while nothing happened. Morris smiled to himself; obviously the attackers were disappointed. As he was thinking along these lines Alex growled, 'They never done this before. Quantrill could have taught 'em better.'

Neither Morris, who knew the name, spoke, nor did Timmy to whom the name Quantrill meant nothing.

By late afternoon Alex's injury was scabbing over and the bleeding had stopped, which was an outward manifestation of a healing process, but as the graze hurt less his ribs hurt more. He said nothing but the way he moved made it clear to his son and Whit Morris that he was in pain.

The raiders did one thing right, they waited until dusk to make another attempt to set the forted-up defenders afoot, and this time they succeeded. Morris and Alex went to the door, their freed horses had been choused southward and as the men listened the sounds diminished.

When the men were back inside Alex said, 'Now they got us cut off. I expect they'll do somethin' bold in the dark.'

Timmy's day-long tension eventually drove him to Whit Morris's bedroll, the only piece of furnishing in the cabin.

His father winked at Morris. They let the boy rest and as night came full down they kept watch, one at the window and the other at the doorless opening.

Morris called out. 'What do you want?' and got back a sarcastic laugh. 'You're sittin' ducks. Is that you, whiskers?'

Morris answered. 'The name's Morris. What do you want?'

'Anybody 'd pay what you did for that buckskin horse's got money. That's what we want. All you'n your friend got.'

Alex called this time. 'Come an' get it!'

He got a quick reply. 'We will. We'll burn you out inside the house.'

Again Alex called back. 'Try it. Green logs don't burn, you dumb son of a bitch.'

Whit took it up. 'Beckwourth?'
'What.'
'There'll be a posse comin' directly.'

This time the sarcastic laugh and reply were blunt.

'You're a liar, whiskers. Nobody can hear gunshots that far. Save your hides, give us the money or we'll leave you up here for the buzzards.'

Alex brushed Whit's arm and spoke quietly. 'Keep 'em talkin'. I got an idea.'

After saying this, Alex Hobart eased closer to the window hole and Morris called to Beckwourth again.

'What we got isn't enough to get shot over.'

This time the answer came in a higher-pitched voice. 'We're not goin' to get shot, you are. Give us the money an' we'll leave.'

This time the voice from the westerly trees was more than Alex Hobart could stand. He called back. 'You lyin' bastard, if we give you the money we'd get killed. You can't afford to have us alive to tell what happened an' get posse riders goin' after you in every direction.'

Alex followed this up with gunfire. He emptied his Winchester, aiming first dead centre, then to the right and left.

No one fired back which made Hobart smile. Whether he'd hit anyone or not he sure-lord had scattered them.

It was another ten minutes before muzzle blasts winked from among the trees. Alex was right, he had scattered them. The return fire was from wide-apart raiders and was more venomous than accurate.

Alex leaned his saddle gun aside. Morris took a long chance and sprayed carbine slugs westerly, belt high.

There was no more gunfire for almost an hour during which Morris used his feet on the inside logs to reach exposed rafters above and Alex watched wearing a scowl, but he said nothing.

Morris sought and did not find a good footing, the rafters were too far apart. He had an advantage, it was a dark night with a measly moon.

As he and Alex Hobart could not discern their attackers yonder among forest giants, neither could the attackers see Whit Morris during his climb nor after he was able to get belly-down atop roofing shakes.

Alex handed up a reloaded Winchester using his arm that did not cause pain when he raised it. He said, 'I loaded it but make them shots count because we got no more .25 – .35 bullets.'

Timmy was awake and as quiet as a church mouse. His father sat on the bedroll beside him and said, 'You're gettin' an education, boy.'

Timmy's voice was high-pitched when he asked his father if they could hold out. Alex had to sit straighter otherwise his chest hurt. 'We'll hold out, boy. If we go to Hell they're goin' with us.'

Timmy made a typical remark. 'If we had them boxes of bullets we got at home . . . '

His father nodded without speaking, hoisted himself to his feet, told Timmy to stay where he was and went over to peer upwards. He saw a purple-dark sky and more stars than a man could count in a life-time, but no sign of Whit Morris.

He raised his voice a little. 'Whit, you all right?'

The reply he got silenced Hobart. 'Be quiet, there's someone comin' from the east.'

Alex cursed himself. They should have made another window cutout in the east wall. They hadn't, so he went after his saddle gun, methodically shucked out spent casings and plugged in fresh loads. When he fumbled for the last belt loop it was empty.

If he used the weapon he'd be one shot shy of a full slide and that would be the end of their carbine ammunition.

The night was so still and hushed they could hear a distant horse whinny which could mean that their saddle animals had not run as far as lowland open country. It could also mean a rider was coming upcountry but neither Morris or Alex Hobart were that hopeful.

Whit Morris fired once, the echo rattled around down below and Timmy would have spoken but his father growled him into silence.

He went over near the bedroll and softly spoke to the man on the roof who had fired. 'Did you get him?'

Whit did not answer but the craggy man and his son could hear him scrambling among the shingles and when Whit levered up another load the extracted casing fell inside. Timmy looked for it but his father didn't. He went back to the window hole.

It was possible to see distant trees without the horses between which had hindered a sighting. Alex speculated that at least one raider was over there but the more he listened to Whit scraping overhead the more he thought that there were at least two of them east of the cabin, something he could only ascertain by going outside which he had no intention of doing.

But his conjecture was flawed and if he had thought about it he would have known it. Why would one of the raiders remain among the trees?

He hadn't. In fact all three raiders were east of the cabin. Hobart made that discovery when a flurry of gunshots erupted.

One man could not have fired that many shots. Above, on the roof, Morris fired back three times with his hand gun, which signified to Alex Hobart that their enemies were close to the cabin.

There was a brief lull in the gunfire before one solitary shot which sounded very close caused Morris on the roof to squirm noiselessly right up until the moment he fell between two rafters and landed on the floor near Timmy.

The boy was petrified. His father turned inward near the doorway to watch Morris struggle to arise and to fall back.

Hobart ripped out a curse and sprang

closer to help Morris arise, and felt sticky warmth on his hands. He told his son to move clear, helped Morris reach the bedroll and eased him down. It was difficult with poor visibility to see the wound so Alex Hobart groped until he found it. Morris had his jaws locked, his breath came in gasps.

The bullet had him up near the hip and because it had been a .45 calibre it made a ragged and gory wound.

Hobart told his son to cut Whit's shirt into strips. Between them they got the shirt off. The only sound on Morris's part was caused by being jerked to get the shirt clear. It was a bitten-back groan.

Alex cut the trouser leg from ankle to the belt line, took a strip of shirting from his son and clamped it over the injury. Within moments it was soaked and soggy. Alex cut higher, through the waistband and belt, exposed the leg, took several more shirting strips from Timmy, who was white to the hairline, which was not discernible in the cabin's gloom, twisted the strips together for strength, got them inches above the wound and used his pistol barrel to twist until most of the bleeding stopped.

He sat back on his heels looking down. When Whit tried to make a sweaty death's-head smile Hobart said, 'Four inches higher, partner, an' there'd be no way to tie it off.'

Whit Morris was weakening fast. Before he lost consciousness he said, 'All three of 'em,' and closed his eyes as he turned loose all over.

Hobart got back upright, dried bloody hands on his trousers and looked at his son. 'Take his pistol. Any loads in it?'

'One.'

'Reload it from his shellbelt.'

Hobart went back in the direction of the door but to one side. A man and a frightened boy against bad odds.

As Timmy approached with Morris's gun dangling, his father jerked his head. 'Mind the window, stay to one side, don't show yourself.'

As Timmy went to obey, his father watched him. He couldn't lose the only thing left that was part of his wife.

Someone hurled a stone against the east wall. Hobart ignored it. If they came it had to be from the front or the westerly window hole.

Moments passed into minutes. There was not a sound until the man with the recognizable voice called again. 'It ain't worth dyin' for, gents. We can put you down whenever we want to. We seen that feller on the roof get hit afore he fell inside. That leaves a man an' a boy. You ready to hand over the money?'

Hobart's answer was more growl than shout. 'You damned fools, there isn't that much money.'

'Is that a fact? Walk out with your hands high an' we'll decide whether there's much money or not.'

This time Hobart didn't answer, he listened. Someone was creeping southward along the east wall. It was impossible not to make even

212

slight sound; aside from shavings and whitlings the ground around there had been ground to dust during the building process.

The stalker was very careful to move one foot at a time and if he'd been wearing moccasins he wouldn't have made a sound, but he was wearing boots.

Alex risked a look over where Timmy was. Sure as Hell was hot they wouldn't all be on the east side. He spoke to his son keeping his voice low. 'Cock the pistol an' wait. Any movement you see — shoot!'

Timmy cocked the six-gun. His father faced forward again. Both he and his son had fully loaded handguns. They also had enough ammunitions left for full reloads.

Whit Morris groaned, not loudly but loudly enough for the sound to carry in the total stillness. Alex Hobart ignored Morris. That stalker was approaching the south-east corner of the house when he halted.

Hobart brought his six-gun up and very gently raised the hammer. It was not a silent action but inside four log walls the way he had done it did not carry more than a foot or two.

He risked another look in his son's direction. Timmy hadn't moved, the gun still dangled at his side, but moments after his father turned back toward the door hole Timmy began to slowly raise his gun.

'Last chance,' Beckwourth called. 'Sixty seconds then the buzzards can have you. Sixty seconds, you mutton head.'

Hobart remained silent. The sixty seconds ran on. How long sixty seconds were was anyone's guess, neither the forted-up defenders nor their attackers owned watches.

More than a minute passed when the gunshot from inside the cabin nearly deafened Alex Hobart. He spun half around. His son was standing stiff as a ramrod facing the window. Outside a man screamed like a wounded eagle.

Hobart spun forward. The stalker was no longer attempting to move soundlessly and this time the sounds were of two men not one.

Hobart got against the west side of the front wall scarcely breathing. He raised the cocked Colt. What happened next was afterwards a source of much head-wagging. Both the bull-necked man and the thin, taller man sprang into the door opening. Both fired into the shadowy gloom, their muzzle blasts lancing red.

Without haste Alex Hobart aimed his first shot slightly higher than a muzzle blast and squeezed the trigger. He immediately hauled back the dog and fired again the same way.

Someone's pistol went off upwards. It was over in seconds but no one moved for a longer period of time. After the last ear-ringing blast lost its echo, Alex stepped clear of the wall looking down.

From the rear of the room an unsteady voice said, 'Alex? *Alex!*'

Hobart answered. 'It's finished, Whit. Go back to sleep.'

The man who had screamed after Timmy's wild shot ran easterly like a deer. If he had been hit, and surely he had been, it must not have been a hard hit otherwise he couldn't have fled.

Hobart leaned, flung away the guns of the men lying sprawled just outside the door, and said, 'Damned fools,' then went over where Timmy was standing, brushed the boy's shoulder with one hand and softly said, 'That one won't be back.'

'Pa, I missed him an' he was close.'

'You didn't miss him, son. He hollered like a gutshot bear.'

Timmy turned. 'Them other two?'

'Son, now them two know somethin' we don't know ... I wish I had the jug.'

12

A Time of change

Hobart crouched beside the bedroll. Morris could make out his face in the gloom. Alex looked tired. Whit said, 'Did you get 'em?'

'Got Beckwourth an' the skinny one. Timmy winged the other one an' he run for the trees. By now he'll be a-horseback. Whit, can't neither of us make the trip. I'm goin' to send Timmy down yonder for help. Your leg's swelling big as a flour sack. Me . . . got a couple of broke or cracked ribs.'

Hobart returned to the window hole where his son was leaning against the wall still holding Morris's six-gun.

His father gently took the gun from him and told him to be extra careful as he went down to Bullhead City for help. His final words to the boy were,

'I expect that one you winged'll be out of the country, but be careful anyway. Here, take the pistol. Can you make it down there?'

Timmy nodded as he asked how Whit Morris was and his father lied, 'He's doin' fine. Son, it's a considerable distance.'

Timmy wanly smiled in the gloom. 'I can make it all right. I'll fetch back help. The lawman, too, Pa?'

'If he's handy. Timmy, mind now; that other son of a bitch is out there somewhere. If you see him . . . '

Timmy's smile lingered. 'I know what to do.'

'Don't give him a chance. Shoot first an' keep shootin'.'

'Pa? Will you be all right?'

'I'll be fine. If there's someone down there who does doctorin' fetch him back . . . Timmy?'

'Pa?'

Hobart laid a hand on his son's shoulder. 'I'm real proud of you. Now go.'

Timmy had to step over the bodies beyond the door. Moments later he passed from the sight of his father who stood in the doorway until there was no longer even any sound.

He went back to the bedroll, sat down with his back to the wall and blew out a rattling sigh. Whit said, 'Next time I'll have a jug handy.'

Hobart looked at the shadowy face nearby and said, 'Won't be no next time, partner.'

Whit's leg hurt less than it ached. Hobart leaned to loosen the tie-off briefly; blood spurted. He retightened the tie-off and wiped his hands on his trousers. As he resumed his leaning position he said, 'Lately I been wrong a lot, but if I was to guess I'd say it'll be until next winter before you can use that leg.' What Hobart thought, but did not mention, was a notion that for as long as Whit Morris lived he'd have a limp.

The predawn chill arrived. Hobart snugged blankets around Whit. The wounded man looked up as he said, 'I got a question, Alex. How did the gov'ment know where to send that letter of pardon to you?'

'The gov'ment didn't,' Hobart replied. 'The writin' on the envelope was my sister's handwritin'. The pardon was mailed to her an' because she knew where I was, she forwarded it.'

'I don't remember you tellin' me you had a sister,' Whit said, and could see the expression on the older man's face when he replied, 'Lots of things I haven't told you, Whit.'

A distant wolf sat back and howled at the spindly moon. If he was calling for a mate he was disappointed. There was no answering call. It was the wrong time of the year.

Whit dozed off and Alex arose to prowl the night and to drag those stiffening obstacles away from the opening.

As time passed and tiredness increased he returned to the cabin, heard something outside a'ways and went to stand in the doorway with his six-gun dangling.

The buckskin horse was out there cropping feed as though he had never left. Hobart smiled. There was one thing about animals; when they formed a strong attachment they went where they last met the cause of it.

Short-backed, halter pulling and whatever else most folks didn't like in a horse, in this case were more than offset.

Alex looked and listened for the other animals until it was clear only the buckskin had returned, then went to the back wall near the bedroll, shoved out his legs, put his handgun within reach and closed his eyes. For years it had been his custom to encourage a good night's sleep by breathing deeply for several minutes. This time he did not do that. For another obvious reason he did not have to. His head dropped forward and he slept like the dead.

Even the sound of ridden horses did not awaken him, but it awakened

Morris, who listened until he was satisfied it was more than one horse and that they were coming single file, which meant they were being ridden. He raised up slightly and rattled Hobart awake.

Alex's first move was to reach for the six-gun, but he didn't raise it as he too listened.

He ached in places he had no idea he had such places, got heavily to his feet, mumbled aside to Whit and went to the doorway.

There were streaks of dawn light touching the mesa. Four horsemen were following a fifth rider. Hobart could make out his son and put up the six-gun as he addressed Morris without taking his eyes off the riders.

'Timmy must've run all the way. Whit? There's a woman with 'em.'

He stepped outside as the horsemen approached. The townsmen looked long at the corpses but Timmy looked at his father and he smiled.

For as long as was required for

the riders to dismount and tie their animals there was nothing said. Hobart recognized the woman, she was the unfriendly, sullen-eyed person who had the café down yonder.

She had saddle-bags with her when she went up to Alex and asked where the man named Morris was. He jerked his head. 'Inside.'

The woman didn't move. 'Are you all right?'

Hobart looked down. 'Maybe some cracked ribs. Morris got hit high in the leg.'

As the woman headed for the cabin, the coarsefeatured, piggy-eyed town constable approached, stopped to consider the corpses and raised his head as he spoke in an inflectionless voice. 'Did you shoot 'em?'

'Yes, both of 'em. There was a third man but he run for it.'

The lawman nodded about that. 'I got him at the jailhouse. He run his horse too hard an' it give out on him. He's got a gash across his back. After the woman patched him up him'n me had a long talk.'

Hobart nodded at one of the constable's companions, the town blacksmith, who nodded back but said nothing. The other two riders were only vaguely familiar to Alex Hobart. They stood beside their animals looking at the dead men. One of them eventually said, 'Hell, that's Sid Beckwourth. He used to come in for supplies for old man Cutter's outfit.'

The speaker did not identify the other dead man, possibly because he was face down. No one made an attempt to turn him over.

Hobart asked why they'd brought the woman and got a reply in the constable's customary unemotional manner.

'That's Ellie Bard from the eatery in town. She does midwifin' an' whatnot. Has, ever since she come here from back East years back. I never asked an' she never said, but sure as we're standin' here she's patched folks up an' is trained in how to do it.'

Alex, who did not like the lawman, said nothing, but he thought a lot. She'd have to be real good to patch up Whit Morris.

One of the riders Hobart could not place walked over and offered a pony. Hobart took it, thanked its owner, dropped down three swallows, handed back the bottle and raised the back of one hand to his eyes. It wasn't whiskey in the bottle, it was brandy, the kind folks used to blend with house paint.

The woman emerged from the house with blood almost to her elbows which everyone but Alex Hobart saw. Alex was staring at something she was carrying. When she saw Hobart's stare, she offered him the doeskin money-belt as she said, 'He wants you to mind it for him until he's up and around. It's his life's savings from selling out a cattle outfit.'

Alex took the belt, draped it over a shoulder and asked the café-woman how Morris was. Her reply was a little dry. 'For what happened to him, he's fine. But he needed stitches. The wound mightn't heal by itself for a very long time, and even then it wouldn't heal properly.' The dark-eyed woman paused before also saying, 'He should be brought to town. Down there I have what I'd need to care for him properly.'

Alex got two vertical lines across his forehead. 'Is it safe to move him?'

The woman answered cryptically. 'No. The bleeding's down to a trickle now. Taking him that far would start it again.'

The woman turned, smiled at Timmy who smiled back, put her back to the corpses and softly said, 'This is beautiful up here . . . what did you say your name was?'

'Hobart. Alex Hobart.'

She stared. 'Alex Hobart. I've heard about you. It's said around Bullhead City that you tried to . . . '

The town constable interrupted. 'Mister Hobart, we ain't set up for haulin' them dead fellers back with us. If you'd bury 'em I'd take it real kindly.'

Hobart looked away from the woman when he replied, 'It'd be a while before I could do that much diggin'.' He looked past the constable. 'Timmy?'

'I can dig the holes, Pa.'

'Constable, my boy'll see to it — for two dollars.'

The phlegmatic town constable's eyes widened. Alex smiled. 'I'd really feel better if you gents take 'em behind your saddles when you leave . . . they're gettin' a tad stiff. Ridin' back the way you come among the trees a man'd have to sidle a lot. Their legs an' arms is most likely stiff by now. Of course, you could break 'em.'

Before Constable Drake could speak, the blacksmith said, 'Not on my horse, Henry,' and another man said the same thing.

Constable Drake gazed balefully at Hobart. 'You killed 'em, we didn't.'

'You're the lawman,' Hobart replied. 'I'm not.'

'In town I can hire grave-diggers for four bits, Mister Hobart.'

Alex conceded. 'That's dirt cheap,' he said. 'Up here it's two dollars a grave.'

'You said two dollars.'

'For a fact I did, Constable. Two dollars *a grave*.'

The lawman looked around and in anticipation his companions shook their heads. Constable Drake groped in a trouser pocket, brought out a crumpled wad of greenbacks and handed four of them to Alex Hobart.

No one said a word as Hobart pocketed the money but the café-woman was close to smiling.

The disgruntled lawman said, 'There's a new regulation in town. There's got to be a certificate of death.'

Hobart stepped over where he had shucked out casings after the gunfight, picked up two and put them in Henry Drake's hand without saying a word.

The woman raised a hand to her mouth to stifle laughter. No one else looked amused. The woman returned to the cabin.

Whit had heard most of what had been said beyond the doorway. He made a shy smile at the woman. He probably wouldn't have felt like doing that if she hadn't got some laudanum down him.

With no sense of either pain nor weakness he said, 'I seen you at the eatery but I don't know your name, ma'am.'

'Eleanor Bard. Folks call me Ellie. Hold still, I want another look at the bandaging.'

'Ma'am, how come you to know about patchin' folks up?'

Without looking up she answered shortly, 'I was a nurse in Philadelphia.'

'Is that where you're from?'

'Yes.'

'Ma'am . . . '

She cut him off with a cold stare. 'One thing I learned to like about the

West is how folks know better than to ask personal questions . . . You should shave.'

He watched her go outside where the men were getting ready to leave. Alex Hobart asked her a question. 'How much would it cost to hire you to ride up here an' look after him?'

Her answer was short. 'I have a café to run.' She went to a horse where Constable Drake was holding the reins, turned and spoke again to Alex Hobart. 'It'll be a long time before he can get around. Keep it clean with fresh bandaging. Don't wrap the wound with old shirts.'

She swung astride, evened up her reins and, as the lawman went to get his horse, she again addressed Alex Hobart. 'If he gets an infection it could kill him.'

Alex made a gesture with both arms. 'We don't have no clean bandagin' nor any medicine except horse liniment.'

She thoughtfully evened up her reins, her companions were already moving. She squeezed the animal and as it passed Alex she said, 'I'll be up tomorrow with medicine and bandaging.'

He smiled. 'If you got room I'd admire havin' you bring along a bottle of whiskey.'

As she rode past without speaking, Alex watched her until she eventually disappeared among the trees, then went inside where Timmy and Whit Morris were quietly conversing. Timmy said, 'All I know is that they said she was real good deliverin' babies, sewin' up cuts and doctorin'.'

Timmy looked up as his father came to stand close and told Whit the café-woman would return tomorrow with what he'd need for his injury, then Alex took his son with him and went outside to dig in soft soil to make graves.

The following day the two Hobarts went horse hunting. Whit ate jerky, drank water from a canteen and lay still smoking and speculating.

The woman hadn't liked the beard

he thought enhanced his appearance. He had a reason for wearing it.

He could see out the opening, could smell wild flowers and grass as well as fir sap and freshly cut wood.

Probably because there was none of the customary noise and movement, birds landed on the roof, even hopped over to peer down. When he would have talked to them they fled.

Timmy and his father returned a little shy of sundown driving loose stock ahead of them. They had returned with more saddle animals, more than they had lost. Two wore saddles and bridles which they dumped near the cabin before taking the animals out where grass was stirrup high.

When they came to the cabin they were hungry. Timmy went out to the stone ring to make a supper fire, his father hunkered beside the bedroll and talked.

'They was down close to open country. The ones wearin' bridles had stepped on their reins, so they're short.

I'll tell you what I think. Two of them horses is branded. The same mark. I think they was stolen from the outfit those fellers worked for.'

Hobart arose, he was tired but he smiled. 'We made a sashay by home an' I brought the jug back with us. It's with the horse gear if you'd like a sip.'

Morris smiled and Hobart went after the jug. When he returned and handed it over, Whit took down a deep breath. Alex Hobart's homemade corn squeezing was mud-coloured and tasted like the wrath of God.

He closed his eyes, swallowed twice and kept his eyes closed as he held out the jug. Very gradually he let his breath out. It was flammable but the effect was almost instantaneous.

Timmy brought supper to Morris after which he and his father went outside to eat. Whit suspected they had brought more than the jug from the homestead because there were peas and carrots on his platter.

The Hobarts left Whit with dusk fading. They would return the following day, which is what they did but as they emerged from the trees they both saw a dozing horse in front of the house. Timmy didn't recognize it but his father did, and estimated that the café-woman must have left Bullhead City before sunrise in order to reach Devil's Den as soon as she obviously had.

There were tendrils of smoke spiralling lazily from within the stone ring. Alex told his son they would hobble the horses out with the other animals and approach the house on foot.

When Alex appeared in the doorway, Whit saw him first and called a greeting. The café-woman glanced up once then looked away.

Alex cleared his throat before saying he and Timmy would care for her horse, turn it out with the others to eat. She spoke without looking up. 'I have no hobbles.'

Hobart's retort was consistent with the reply a man would make who had encountered this condition before. 'We'll make a pair out of what's left of Whit's shirt,' and led the way back in the direction of the grazing animals carrying the soiled and torn shirt.

The woman went to the window hole to watch and returned to the bedroll with a wise comment. 'Living like they do I suppose they've learned to innovate, to make-do.'

Whit nodded. 'He's a good man an' he's done a fine job with the boy.'

'He doesn't have a wife?'

'She's dead.'

'I'm sorry to hear that . . . you?'

'Yes'm, I'm sorry about that too.'

She looked directly at him. *Men! Strong as oak and twice as thick.* 'I meant, your wife.'

'Never had one,' Whit replied. 'Alex'll sure thank you for bringin' the bottle of whiskey.'

'You didn't taste it.'

'No ma'am. I never cared for the taste . . . do you like it?'

She was examining his wound when

she replied, 'No! My husband drank himself to death.'

He couldn't find any appropriate words so he remained silent until she was satisfied with the new bandage and its scent of disinfectant and was ready to arise, then he said, 'We been workin' on this cabin a long time.'

She slowly turned as though seeing the inside for the first time and eventually said, 'It's — wonderful.' She was looking out the window when she also repeated something she'd said earlier, 'It's beautiful up here.'

He grinned. 'It's haunted.'

She turned, looking down. 'So I've heard . . . Is it?'

'No; not that I know of an' I've been up here most of the spring an' summer. You know what an echo box is?'

She shook her head so he explained. When he had finished she went slowly to collect the things she'd brought, such as scissors and soap, tucked them into a pair of saddle-bags and turned again to look at him.

'If I brought a razor next time . . . ?'

He grinned, scratched the beard. 'I'd shave it off.'

She was holding the saddle-bags still looking at him when she asked what he intended to do on his homestead.

He answered without hesitation. 'Build a log place for my horse, do a little huntin' an' fishin'. Maybe someday make a storage shed, a pole corral.'

'And a chicken house?'

'Later, when I get the time. Bein' one-legged is goin' to slow me down.'

'You have the Hobarts . . . '

'They got their own place to look after, ma'am.'

She lingered, saddle-bags in hand, steadily regarding him. 'Your name is Whitman?' she asked.

'It's Whitman, but they call me Whit.'

'Would it be all right if I called you Whit?'

'I'd like for you to, ma'am.'

'Would it bother you to call me Ellie?'

His face felt warm. 'Wouldn't bother me at all.'

'Whit?'

'Yes'm?'

This time she hung fire before speaking but did not take her eyes off his face. 'Whit . . . would it bother you to have a woman help you make the barn, the corral an' the chicken house?'

Alex and Timmy appearing in the doorway saved him from having to answer. She nodded to the Hobarts, shouldered the saddle-bags and went out to catch her horse, rig out and ride through the warming midday.

Hobart considered Morris, turned to watch the woman pass from sight in forest gloom, looked back and said, 'She's a good nurse, Whit.'

Morris nodded.

'We'll leave the bottle here, take the jug an' head for home. Whit?'

'Yes.'

'Is she comin' back?'

'I expect so. I think she might.'

Hobart studied the man on the bedroll. 'Do what she says. We'll ride over now'n then . . . Whit?'

'Alex — Timmy — I owe you more'n money could pay.'

Hobart rubbed a stubbly jaw. 'You done more for us than we done for you. Timmy'n me is right proud to have you for a neighbour.' Hobart looked up where sunlight was shining through. 'We'll come over when we get caught up at home an' finish the roof. Do like I said, Whit, whatever she tells you to do — partner, do it.'

After the Hobarts left, Whit looked up for a long time. He'd never in his life heard of a female woman draw-knifing logs, splitting sugar pine shakes or helping make a pole corral. Maybe she was just saying those things.

He slept like a log until close to sunrise when a solitary gunshot awakened him. He reached for his gun and waited for someone to appear in the doorway.

It was a long wait during which he

heard horses moving. His first thought was that someone was stealing the saddle animals and he was helpless to prevent it.

The next sound was of boots approaching the house. He cocked the six-gun and waited.

When she blocked out doorway light, saw the cocked, aimed gun, she said, 'There were some wolves stalking the horses,' came inside and dropped a pair of saddle-bags beside the bedroll.

He had only seen her wearing dresses that hung like feed sacks with her dark hair combed but splayed in back.

Today she had a midriff belt so the gunny sack effect was lacking and someway she had made a wolftail braid up the back of her head, and she smiled.

He felt foolish holding the gun. He eased down the dog and put the weapon aside. He hadn't expected her — he had hoped hard but two days in a row . . .

She knelt to examine the bandaging,

said, 'It has to be changed.'

'You just changed it yestiddy, ma'am.'

She leaned to look straight at him. 'Ellie, remember? Not ma'am — Ellie. And the bandage should be changed every day and disinfected. It's a pure miracle it's not infected after that soiled shirt it was wrapped in. Hold still, when I sprinkle this powder it's going to burn. *Hold still.*'

He nodded without smiling. The white powder burned like fire. From his expression she asked if he'd like something from the bottle and he wagged his head.

She looked around as she emptied the saddle-bags which had been filled with tinned items like peaches, spiced beef, sugar, coffee and salt. 'Whit, before the barn and other things, you need a table, beds built along the wall, chairs and a decent place to cook.'

He offered no argument except to say he had no tools to make those things with and also lacked the skill.

She went to the window hole and leaned there. 'Whit, if I can do those things so can you.'

'Make chairs an' . . . '

She faced around with sunlight at her back. 'Tomorrow I'll bring the tools. They belonged to my husband. I helped him make things.'

Whit was again unable to find appropriate words so he said nothing. She came over, sat on her heels and looked steadily at him.

'Whit?'

'Uh — Ellie?'

'I didn't mean to be real forward yesterday.'

This time he found words. 'Was you forward? I lay a spell last night thinkin' how nice it'd be havin' you up here working with me. Ellie?'

She waited until he said, 'You got to help me.'

'All right. It's bothering you me being in the cabin. I'll bring my bedroll and sleep outside.'

His eyes widened and hardened. 'No,

ma'am, not on your life. I'll sleep outside.'

'You can't walk.'

'Then I'll crawl.'

She softly laughed, shot up to her feet and said, 'We'll see. I'll make us something to eat, but that stone ring . . . '

'I'll make a rock stove in a corner.'

'Do you know how, Whit?'

'I'll figure it out. Do you know how it's done?'

She smiled as she replied, 'No, but between us we can do it. Whit, I've got to get back.'

'How about the café?'

She made a little shrug. 'I'll close it. I'll be back in the morning.'

Other titles in the
Linford Western Library

THE CROOKED SHERIFF
John Dyson

Black Pete Bowen quit Texas with a burning hatred of men who try to take the law into their own hands. But he discovers that things aren't much different in the silver mountains of Arizona.

THEY'LL HANG BILLY
FOR SURE:
Larry & Stretch
Marshall Grover

Billy Reese, the West's most notorious desperado, was to stand trial. From all compass points came the curious and the greedy, the riff-raff of the frontier. Suddenly, a crazed killer was on the loose — but the Texas Trouble-Shooters were there, girding their loins for action.

RIDERS OF RIFLE RANGE
Wade Hamilton
Veterinarian Jeff Jones did not like open warfare — but it was there on Scrub Pine grass. When he diagnosed a sick bull on the Endicott ranch as having the contagious blackleg disease, he got involved in the warfare — whether he liked it or not!

BEAR PAW
Nevada Carter
Austin Dailey traded two cows to a pair of Indians for a bay horse, which subsequently disappeared. Tracks led to a secret hideout of fugitive Indians — and cattle thieves. Indians and stockmen co-operated against the rustlers. But it was Pale Woman who acted as interpreter between her people and the rangemen.

THE WEST WITCH
Lance Howard

Detective Quinton Hilcrest journeys west, seeking the Black Hood Bandits' lost fortune. Within hours of arriving in Hags Bend, he is fighting for his life, ensnared with a beautiful outcast the town claims is a witch! Can he save the young woman from the angry mob?

GUNS OF THE PONY EXPRESS
T. M. Dolan

Rich Zennor joined the Pony Express venture at the start, as second-in-command to tough Denning Hartman. But Zennor had the problems of Hartman believing that they had crossed trails in the past, and the fact that he was strongly attached to Hartman's Indian girl, Conchita.

BLACK JO OF THE PECOS
Jeff Blaine

Nobody knew where Black Josephine Callard came from or whither she returned. Deputy U.S. Marshal Frank Haggard would have to exercise all his cunning and ability to stay alive before he could defeat her highly successful gang and solve the mystery.

RIDE FOR YOUR LIFE
Johnny Mack Bride

They rode west, hoping for a new start. Then they met another broken-down casualty of war, and he had a plan that might deliver them from despair. But the only men who would attempt it would be the truly brave — or the desperate. They were both.

THE NIGHTHAWK
Charles Burnham

While John Baxter sat looking at the ruin that arsonists had made of his log house, a stranger rode into the yard. Baxter and Walt Showalter partnered up and re-built the house. But when it was dynamited, they struck back — and all hell broke loose.

MAVERICK PREACHER
M. Duggan

Clay Purnell was hopeful that his posting to Capra would be peaceable enough. However, on his very first day in town he rode into trouble. Although loath to use his .45, Clay found he had little choice — and his likeness to a notorious bank robber didn't help either!

SIXGUN SHOWDOWN
Art Flynn

After years as a lawman elsewhere, Dan Herrick returned to his old Arizona stamping ground to find that nesters were being driven from their homesteads by ruthless ranchers. Before putting away his gun once and for all, Dan forced a bloody and decisive showdown.

RIDE LIKE THE DEVIL!
Sam Gort

Ben Trunch arrived back on the Big T only to find that land-grabbing was in progress. He confronted Luke Fletcher, saloon-keeper and town boss, with what was happening, and was immediately forced to ride for his life. But he got the chance to put it all right in the end.

SLOW WOLF AND DAN FOX:
Larry & Stretch
Marshall Grover
The deck was stacked against an innocent man. Larry Valentine played detective, and his investigation propelled the Texas Trouble-Shooters into a gun-blazing fight to the finish.

BRANAGAN'S LAW
Alan Irwin
To Angus Flint, the valley was his domain and he didn't want any new settlers. But Texas Ranger Jim Branagan had other ideas. Could he put an end to Flint's tyranny for good?

THE DEVIL RODE A PINTO
Bret Rey
When a settler is cut to ribbons in a frenzied attack, Texas Ranger Sam Buck learns that the killer is Rufus Berry, known as The Devil. Sam stiffens his resolve to kill or capture Berry and break up his gang.